HARLEQUIN®
Presents

What can you expect in Harlequin Presents?

Passionate relationships

Revenge and redemption

Emotional intensity

Seduction

Escapist, glamorous settings from around the world

New stories every month

The most handsome and successful heroes

Scores of internationally bestselling writers

Find all this in our November books—on sale now!

Lee Wilkinson

THE BEJEWELLED BRIDE

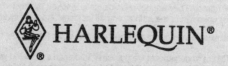

TORONTO • NEW YORK • LONDON
AMSTERDAM • PARIS • SYDNEY • HAMBURG
STOCKHOLM • ATHENS • TOKYO • MILAN • MADRID
PRAGUE • WARSAW • BUDAPEST • AUCKLAND

ISBN-13: 978-0-373-12586-9
ISBN-10:   0-373-12586-0

THE BEJEWELLED BRIDE

First North American Publication 2006.

www.eHarlequin.com

Printed in U.S.A.

All about the author...
Lee Wilkinson

LEE WILKINSON attended an all-girls school, where her teachers, often finding her daydreaming, declared that she "lived inside her own head," and that is still largely true today. Until her marriage, she had a variety of jobs, ranging from PA to a departmental manager, to modeling swimsuits and underwear.

As an only child and avid reader from an early age, she began writing when she, her husband and their two children moved to Derbyshire. She started with short stories and magazine serials before going on to write romances for Harlequin Mills & Boon.

A lover of animals—after losing Kelly, her adored German shepherd—she has a rescue dog named Thorn, who looks like a pit bull and acts like a big softy, apart from when the postman calls. Then he has to be restrained, otherwise he goes berserk and shreds the mail.

Traveling has always been one of Lee's main pleasures. After crossing Australia and America in a motor home, and traveling round the world on two separate occasions, she still, periodically, suffers from itchy feet.

She enjoys walking and cooking, log fires and red wine, music and the theater, and still much prefers books to television—both reading and writing them.

CHAPTER ONE

BETHANY glanced around her. The scenery on the high mountain pass was awesomely bleak and beautiful in the pearly grey light of an early February afternoon. For the first few miles, while the pass had run fairly straight and level between rock-strewn fells, she had seen a black Range Rover in the rear-view mirror. But over the last half mile or so it must have turned off into a side valley, because now she had the road to herself.

When she had set off to Bosthwaite earlier in the day to visit Mrs Deramack and look at some antiques, she had taken the main road but had taken this lonely route back especially to see more of the wild and rugged grandeur she remembered well from her one previous visit to the Lake District.

As she drove however, she thought back to that wonderful visit and remembered a lean, good-looking face with brilliant eyes and a mouth with the kind of male beauty that tied her insides in knots.

A face that had stayed fresh in her mind for the past six years.

Quiet and shy, she had been just seventeen at the time and on a family holiday with her parents. Returning from the west coast of Scotland, they had decided to spend one night in Cumbria on their way back to London.

They had been staying in Dundale End, and after dinner that

evening, encouraged by their landlady, 'You must go, my dears, everyone will be there…' they had gone to a concert at the small village hall. In front of a makeshift stage, rows of chairs had been arranged in a semi-circle, and it had been there, sitting on an un-comfortable plastic chair in the centre of the second row, that she had fallen in love for the first time. Love at first sight. The hot, crazy kind of love that had turned her chest into a bell and her heart into a clapper.

She had watched him walk in, tall and broad across the shoul-ders, casually dressed, he had an air of quiet confidence. Some-where in his early twenties, he was a man not a boy, with a strong-boned face, thick corn-coloured hair and light, brilliant eyes.

With him had been an elderly couple and a girl about his own age, who addressed him as Joel.

Joel… Bethany had hugged the name to her as though it was some precious gift.

He exchanged greetings with many of the people there, which suggested he was a local. Bethany had wished fervently that she and her parents were staying here instead of going back to London the next day.

Try as she would, her eyes had been drawn to him more often than to the stage. On one occasion she had found him staring back at her with a quiet intensity that made heat spread through her entire body. Feeling her cheeks flame, she had looked hastily away, her curtain of long dark hair swinging forward, hiding her embarrassment.

As the show came to an end, finishing with prolonged and hearty applause, she had kept her attention fixed firmly on the stage.

Perhaps when everyone was on their way out they might meet, might exchange a word. Lovely evening… Are you on holiday…? But when she'd glanced back, the little group had gone. She'd felt bitterly disappointed.

Although she had told herself it was ridiculous to long for something that only *might* have happened, she had thought and dreamt about him for months.

The memory of that past innocent adoration warmed her and for a few precious seconds took her mind off this which was turning out to be a disaster.

In more ways than one.

That morning, after a poor night's sleep and an uncomfortable half hour spent sitting opposite her silent, still-angry boss, Tony, while they ate breakfast at the Dundale Inn, she had taken the main road to the valley of Bosthwaite to see Mrs Deramack.

It was, she had discovered, a dead-end valley, and the tiny, isolated hamlet of Bosthwaite was made up of a few widely scattered houses and a farm.

Finding the road—which was little more than a track—ran through the farmyard, she had stopped to ask directions.

After warning her, 'Old Mrs Deramack's a bit... you know...' Apparently at a loss for words, the farmer had tapped his forehead with a gnarled finger, before pointing out Bosthwaite House.

Bethany soon realized what he'd meant when the old lady informed her that though Joseph, her husband, had passed away some five years ago, he was still with her and would need to agree on the price of anything she parted with.

The antiques she wanted to sell were stored in the freezing cold, badly lit attic, and while she hovered at the bottom of the attic stairs talking to her husband as though he was still alive and with them, Bethany had gone through what seemed endless boxes and cartons.

When, chilled to the bone and cramped from so much squatting, her throat dry, clogged with the dust of ages, she had finished the last box, she pushed back a loose strand of dark hair and admitted defeat.

In an attempt to soften the blow, she had told the old lady that though there was nothing amongst her treasures that Feldon Antiques would be prepared to buy, there were other local dealers who might be interested. She had written down the names of two of them before getting into her car and driving away.

When she reached an old white-walled pub called The Drunken Pig, she had stopped to wash her face and hands and re-coil her long dark hair before ordering a refreshing pot of tea and an omelette.

While she ate she had studied her map and decided to take the mountain pass back to Dundale, rather than the main road.

From the start the landscape had been dramatic, but now it had become even more spectacular. On the left was a towering rock face and on the right, an abyss, as the ground dropped away precipitously.

A lot sooner than she had expected, the clear air had become hazy and twilight had started to creep in, while grey swirling mist began to hide the tops of the highest peaks.

She switched on the car's headlights and on a road way down in the valley below saw an answering gleam. Just that distant light, a reminder that she wasn't totally alone, was reassuring.

Even so, she found herself wondering a shade uneasily if she had been wise to take this deserted switchback route—though the Lakeland scenery was truly magnificent, and she loved it.

A love of the country that Tony Feldon, her boss, and owner of Feldon Antiques since the death of his father the previous year, had signally failed to share.

He had made no secret of the fact that he was a dedicated city man and couldn't wait to get back to London and 'civilization'.

When they had drawn up outside the Dundale Inn the previous night, he had glanced around at the dark fells and shuddered. 'It looks like the back of beyond! When I booked I should have made sure it was in town…'

She wondered why he'd booked it himself rather than leaving it to Alison, his general dogsbody.

'If we're forced to stay in this God-forsaken spot for two nights, it had better be worth it,' he muttered half under his breath.

'I'm sure it will be.' Hoping to keep him in a reasonably good mood, she added, 'There are some very fine lots listed in Greendales' preview catalogue.'

Taking their overnight bags from the car boot, he handed Bethany hers and agreed, 'That's true.'

As she followed him into the hotel and across the deserted lobby to the empty reception desk, he muttered, 'God, what a dump! It looks as if we're the only people staying here.'

'Well it *is* the middle of the week and out of season,' she pointed out.

He dropped his case on the carpet and brought his hand down hard on the brass bell that squatted on the desk like a metal toad. 'It might be the middle of the week and out of season,' he said irritably, 'but the blasted place is supposed to be *open*.'

Ignoring his bad temper and the scowl that marred his darkly handsome features, Bethany went on, 'And from what Mrs Deramack said when I spoke to her on the phone, it sounds as if she has some very good pieces of silver and porcelain.'

'Well, if she has, let's hope the old biddy doesn't realize *how* good, or she'll no doubt want the earth for them.'

'Do you intend to go and see her yourself?'

'No. I had a quick glance at the map. It's quite a way to Bosthwaite Valley, and I'll have more than enough on. I'll get a taxi to Greendales and you can take the car.

'If you think any of the items Mrs Deramack wants to sell are in our line, don't say too much and don't put a price on them. I'll do the negotiating myself, even if it means staying up here an extra day…'

Bethany frowned. His failure to give her a free hand rankled. She had worked for James Feldon, Tony's father, since she had left school at eighteen, and after his sudden and fatal heart attack, she had missed him a great deal.

She had liked and trusted the old man as much as she disliked and distrusted his son. His conviction that women were fair game made her hackles rise, as did his frequent suggestions— since Devlin had been wiped from the picture—that if she loosened up they could 'have a little fun together'.

So far she had managed to keep him at arm's length without too much bad blood, but if he didn't soon get the message and back off she would have to leave.

It was a depressing thought.

She still liked her job and when she wasn't actually travelling the shop was within easy walking distance of the flat in Belgravia that she shared with a friend.

Added to that, while she was working she was not only saving hard but buying up small items with a view to one day starting her own business.

Glancing round the still deserted lobby, Tony banged the bell a second time with unnecessary violence. 'Where the devil is everyone?'

A moment later an elderly woman appeared. 'I'm sorry if I've kept you waiting, but the desk clerk has gone home ill and there's no one to take his place… You have booked?'

'Yes, for two nights. The name's Feldon.'

Opening the register at what appeared to be an almost empty page, she confirmed, 'Ah, yes, here we are… Mr and Mrs Feldon. A double room on the ground floor. Number five.'

As she handed over the key, Bethany came to life. 'There's been some mistake,' she announced distinctly. 'I'm *not* Mrs Feldon, and I need a separate room.'

Catching a glimpse of Tony's furious face, she knew there had been no mistake. That was why he had made the booking himself, and that was what he had meant when he'd said, 'It had better be worth it'.

'Oh, I'm sorry,' the woman apologized. 'Well there's a single just down the corridor. Number nine, if that'll do.'

'That will do fine, thanks,' Bethany assured her crisply and, taking the key, marched in the direction the woman had indicated.

'Damn it all, Bethany,' Tony complained, following her to her door. 'Why did you have to insist on another room?'

She turned to face him, her clear grey eyes sparkling with anger. 'Perhaps it hasn't occurred to you that I don't *want* to go to bed with you?'

He was quite taken back. 'Why not? Plenty of other women do.'

Bethany raised her chin and replied, 'Then you should have brought one of them.'

'I wish I had, rather than bringing a prim and proper little Miss like you,' he snarled angrily.

As she turned away he said more moderately, 'Look, I'm sorry. Change your mind. God knows we could use some fun in a hole like this.'

Bethany was furious. 'For the last time, I don't sleep around, and if you don't stop pestering me I'll be forced to hand in my notice.'

She was invaluable to him and, reluctant to lose her, he muttered, 'There's no need to go to those lengths.' Then, petulantly, 'I don't know why you can't loosen up a bit. You're too old to act like some shrinking virgin. And it's not as if you're still engaged to that Devlin bloke…'

It had been some six weeks before their wedding when, returning early from a business trip to Paris, Bethany had dropped in to Devlin's flat and discovered him in bed with another woman.

Unable to believe his pleas that it had been a spur of the moment thing and would never happen again, she had given him back his ring and walked out.

'Just because you're still angry and bitter at the way he treated you,' Tony went on, 'it doesn't mean you have to take it out on all men.'

When she just looked at him coldly, he taunted, 'If you hadn't been so frigid he wouldn't have needed another woman...' When his cruel jokes elicited no response from her he swung on his heel, and a moment later she heard the slam of his bedroom door.

As she remembered Tony Feldon's harsh comments her mind wandered back to her broken engagement to Devlin that he had callously mentioned. She *had* been both angry and bitter at first. But she had soon discovered, or rather *realized,* that while her pride had been trampled on, her heart was virtually intact. And in retrospect she could see that she had only imagined herself in love with Devlin. In fact she'd only really been drawn to him in the first place because he reminded her a little of the blond stranger she had adored at seventeen...

A sudden savage wrench at the steering wheel and a thumping judder brought her back to the present with a shock.

Her heart in her mouth, she dragged the wheel over and steered to the side of the road away from the steep drop into the valley below.

On shaking legs she climbed out to find—as she had feared—that her nearside front tyre had burst.

Well, she would have to do something about it, and fast. It

was rapidly getting dark and the swirls of mist had changed to thick swathes that were now shrouding the peaks and threatening to roll down and engulf the pass.

Shivering in her fine wool suit, she pulled on her short jacket before going round to open the boot. Lifting the inner cover, she took out a jack, the spare wheel, the wheel brace and a foot-pump.

Though so far she had never been forced to change a wheel, when she had bought her first old banger, her father had insisted on her learning how to.

Now she was grateful. Only it didn't seem to be as easy as she remembered.

She was still struggling to put the jack in place when, miraculously, headlights appeared over the crest of the previous rise. A moment later a big black Range Rover, like the one that had followed her earlier, drew to a halt a few yards away.

As she straightened, a tall well-built man with fair hair got out.

Though she was dazzled by the lights, and with his back to them his face was in shadow, there seemed to be something oddly familiar about him.

'Need some help?' he asked.

He had an attractive voice, she noted, low-pitched and cultured with no trace of a local accent.

'Please,' she said gratefully.

The air was damp and raw and, clenching her teeth to prevent them chattering, she watched his broad back while he proceeded to change the wheel with a deft efficiency she could only admire.

Then, having tested the tyre pressure he put some air in with the foot-pump, observing, 'That ought to do it,' before stowing everything back in the boot and closing it.

'Thank you very much. I can't tell you how grateful I am.'

He wiped his hands on a handkerchief he'd taken from the pocket of his leather car-coat and, turning towards his own vehicle, said easily, 'I'm glad to have been of help.'

As the headlights shone full on him, for the first time she saw his face clearly. It was the face that had haunted her for the past six years.

No, it couldn't be! It was far too much of a coincidence. But even while she told herself it couldn't be *him*, she knew it was. And once again he was going to walk out of her life.

'I don't know what I would have done if you hadn't come along,' she said desperately.

'I'm quite sure you would have managed...' Then, briskly, 'I suggest we get going while we can still see the road.'

In the short time it had taken him to change the wheel the mist had begun to close in with ominous speed, rolling down the mountainside and starting to obscure the drop into the valley below.

A combination of cold, desolation and fear made Bethany shiver.

As though sensing that fear and desolation, he paused and asked, 'Do you know the pass at all?'

'No,' she answered in a small voice.

'In that case I'm going to suggest we team up.' He waited for her nod of assent before adding, 'My name's Joel McAlister.'

Her heart leapt in her chest, making her sound breathless, as she said, 'Mine's Bethany Seaton.'

'Where are you heading for, Miss Seaton?' His rich, smooth voice melted her heart.

Somewhat nervously, she replied. 'I'm staying at the Dundale Inn.'

'I'm heading for the Dundale Valley myself, though judging by how fast the mist's closing in, it's my bet we're not going to get that far.'

'Oh...'

Perhaps he mistook her little exclamation of excitement for panic, because he added quickly, 'But don't worry. If we can make it to the foot of Dunscar, which is about a mile away, there's a small hotel there. It's closed for the winter, but I understand the caretaker lives on the premises.' He went on automatically, 'Now, let's get moving. As it's too narrow here for me to get past, we'll have to take your car.'

Turning off his own vehicle's lights, he added, 'I'd better drive, as I know the road.'

When she made no demur, he opened the passenger door for her, then slid behind the wheel.

Bethany was barely able to see anything except the mist reflecting back the dipped headlights, yet he drove with a careful confidence that was reassuring. Though, truth to tell, rather than worrying about their safety, her thoughts centred on the fact that fate had brought him back into her life.

She was being given a second chance.

The chance.

At seventeen, she would have been too young.

But now, at twenty-three to his twenty-seven—twenty-eight? the timing was perfect.

Unless he was already married?

No! She pushed the awful thought away.

She and this stranger, who was no stranger, were *meant* to be together. She had never been more sure of anything in her whole life.

While they made their way down to Dunscar, her heart beating fast, she studied his profile in the glow from the dashboard.

His nose was straight, his jaw strong, the curve of brow and sweep of long lashes, several shades darker than his hair. At the corner of his mouth was a small dent, too masculine to be called a dimple, but surely it would become one when he smiled...

'Think I'm trustworthy?' Both his words and his voice held a hint of amusement.

Looking hastily away, she said as lightly as possible, 'I certainly hope so. Though it's a bit late to worry about it.'

When he said nothing further, she observed, 'You're obviously very familiar with this area, yet you don't have a local accent.'

He shook his head. 'No.'

'So you don't live around here?' Bethany toyed with the strap of her handbag, her nervous excitement getting the better of her.

'No. I'm based in London.'

Bethany breathed a sigh of relief. That was good news. Though London was a big place, it meant he was closer at hand than if he'd lived in Cumbria.

'Are you up here on business?' she asked.

He smiled wryly. 'You could say that…'

When he made no further attempt at conversation, afraid of spoiling his concentration, she relapsed into silence and, unwilling to be caught staring at him again, looked resolutely ahead.

After a while he remarked, 'Here we are,' and, turning left into grey nothingness, brought the car to a halt and doused the lights.

At first all Bethany could see was mist pressing damply against the windscreen, then ahead and to the right she saw a faint glimmer of light.

He came round to help her out and, an arm at her waist, steered her towards the dark bulk of the hotel and the glow of a lighted window.

Just that casual touch seemed to burn through her clothing, setting every nerve in her body tingling and robbing her of breath.

When they reached what seemed to be a small annex, the window lit, Bethany could see now, by an oil lamp standing on the windowsill, he stepped forward and knocked on the door.

It opened almost immediately, letting out a slanting beam of yellow light, and an elderly man in shirtsleeves and a pullover peered at them, his face startled.

'I'm sorry to disturb you, but we need a couple of rooms for the night,' Joel told him.

'The hotel's closed,' the caretaker said shortly. 'You'll have to go somewhere else.'

'Unfortunately that's not possible. The mist is much too thick.'

'The hotel's closed,' the man repeated doggedly, and made as if to slam the door.

Joel stepped forward and held it, saying something quietly but decidedly that Bethany didn't catch.

'All the rooms are shut up and there's no heating on in the main part,' was the surly reply.

'Well, I'm quite sure you can find us something,' Joel insisted pleasantly. 'In an old place like this there must surely be a room with a fireplace?'

'The manageress lives on the premises while the hotel's open, so there's *her* room. But the bed's not made up and the generator's not working, so there's no electricity…'

'Perhaps you'll show us?'

Grumbling about the cold and damp, and being scarcely able to walk for his rheumatism, the caretaker turned away.

Bethany noticed that Joel kept his foot in the door until the man returned, wearing a jacket and with a bunch of keys and a torch.

He closed the door behind him and, limping a little, led the way through the mist to a side entrance which gave on to a small tiled lobby.

The dank air seemed even colder inside than out.

At the end of a short corridor he opened a door and flashed the torch around a good-sized room furnished as a bedsitter.

They glimpsed a divan bed, a basket piled with logs next to a stone fireplace, a wooden table and chairs, a couple of deep armchairs and, through a door that was standing a little ajar, a tiled bathroom.

'This will do fine,' Joel assured him briskly. 'A couple of pillows, a few blankets and a candle or two are all we'll need.'

'There's bedding and towels in the cupboard and an oil lamp and matches on the chest of drawers,' the caretaker said grudgingly.

'Thanks.' Some notes changed hands before Joel suggested, 'Perhaps you could manage a bite to eat and a hot drink for the lady?'

The man stuffed the notes in his trouser pocket and, sounding somewhat mollified, said, 'I'll see what I can do.' He went, leaving them in total darkness.

As Bethany hesitated uncertainly, Joel's level voice ordered, 'Stay where you are until I've located the matches.'

A moment later she heard the brush of a footfall as he moved unerringly through the blackness, then the scrape and flare of a match.

With an ease that seemed to speak of long practice, he lit the oil lamp, adjusted the flame and replaced the glass chimney. In a moment the room was filled with golden light.

His clothes—smart casuals—looked expensive, his shoes handmade, but, taking no heed of either, he squatted by the hearth and began to set the fire.

She watched as his long well-shaped hands placed first sticks and then split logs on a bed of flaming kindling.

Glancing up, he said, 'You're shivering. Come and get warm.'

Needing no further encouragement, though truth to tell the shivering was due as much to excitement as cold, she went and sat in the low armchair he'd pulled closer to the fire.

Putting her big suede shoulder bag on the floor by the chair, she stretched her numb hands to the leaping flames.

'Feet cold?' he queried, looking at her suede fashion boots.

'Frozen,' she admitted.

Piling more logs on, he suggested, 'They'll get warm a lot quicker if you take your boots off.'

Recognizing the truth of that, she tried to pull them off but they were high and close-fitting and her hands had pins and needles.

'Let me.' Crouching on his haunches, he eased off first one and then the other, before rubbing each foot between his palms.

His touch scattered her wits and made her pulses race. At a deeper level it also made her feel cared for, cherished, and at that moment she would have lost her heart to him, if it hadn't been his already.

Gazing at his bent head, she noticed that his thick fair hair still had minute droplets of water clinging to it. She wanted to dry it and cradle his head to her breast.

'That better?' he asked when he'd rubbed some life back into her slim feet.

'Much better, thank you,' she answered huskily.

'Good.'

He had an olive-toned skin at odds with his fairness, and a smile that almost stopped her heart. As he looked into her face she saw that his eyes weren't the pale blue she had imagined, but a light silvery green. Fascinating eyes...

He rose to his feet just as the door opened and the caretaker returned, a torch in one hand and a plastic carrier bag in the other.

Plonking the bag down on the kitchen counter, the man said shortly, 'There's everything you should need in here. The cooker runs on bottled gas and you'll find a kettle and crockery in the cupboard.'

'Thanks… And goodnight,' Joel said.

With a grunt, the man turned and shambled away.

The thought of a hot drink was a welcome one and Bethany had started to rise when Joel ordered, 'Stay where you are and get warm. I'll rustle up a drink and a sandwich.'

Devlin, worried about protecting his macho image, would have sat down to be waited on, Bethany thought. But Joel, confident about his masculinity, clearly had no worries on that score.

Within a minute the gas was lit, the kettle was on and two mugs were waiting.

When he had closed the curtains, shutting out the grey mist that pressed like a wet grey blanket against the glass, Joel began to unpack the carrier. There was a jar of instant coffee, a plastic carton of milk, a tub of sunflower spread, an unopened pack of cheese and a small sliced loaf.

'Hardly a feast,' he commented, 'but quite adequate, so long as you like cheese and coffee and you don't take sugar.'

'I do, and I don't,' she answered.

He gave her a lazy smile that made her heart quicken and, taking off his short car-coat, tossed it over a chair. 'In that case we don't have a problem.'

As soon as the kettle started to sing, he made the coffee and handed her one of the steaming mugs.

Sipping it gratefully, she watched while, with cool efficiency, he made a plate of sandwiches and, carrying that and two smaller plates over to the hearth, put them on a low table.

The heat of the coffee banishing the last lingering inner coldness, she said, 'I don't think I need this any longer,' and, rising to her feet, made to take off her coat.

He helped her off with it, then, pulling up a chair, joined her in front of what was now a blazing fire and, offering the plate of sandwiches, urged, 'Do make a start.'

'I'm not very hungry.'

When he continued to hold the plate, though she felt too pleasantly agitated to eat, she took a sandwich just to show willing.

'That's better.' He smiled at her.

His teeth gleamed white and even and his smile held such charm that her heart began to beat faster.

Despite the emotional upheaval, after the first few bites her usual healthy appetite kicked in and she found herself enjoying the simple fare. Or, rather, enjoying the fact that she was sitting in front of a blazing fire sharing a plate of sandwiches with the man who had lived in her heart and mind and dreams for so long.

It was almost too wonderful to be true, and she felt like pinching herself to make sure that the whole thing wasn't just another dream.

CHAPTER TWO

'MORE?' Joel queried when the plate was empty.

Replete, Bethany shook her head with a little sigh of contentment.

Noting the sigh, he raised a well-marked brow and teased, 'That bad, huh?'

'As a matter of fact I've thoroughly enjoyed them,' she said, made breathless by his teasing smile.

'I thought at first that you might be too concerned to eat.'

'Concerned?'

'About spending the night with a total stranger.'

He wasn't a total stranger. She had known him for six years. But she could hardly tell him that. He would think she was mad.

Aware of his eyes on her, she said jerkily, 'I'm not at all concerned.'

'You seem a little… shall we say… flustered?'

Not knowing quite what to say to that, she remained silent until he queried, 'So what brings you to these parts?'

'I'm here on business.'

The mention of business broke through the spell his presence wove, reminding her that she ought to let Tony know she couldn't get back.

Reaching for her bag, she took out her mobile.

Joel gave her an enquiring look.

'I must just call the Dundale Inn and let Tony know I can't get back tonight.'

'I'm afraid you'll be wasting your time,' Joel told her. 'You won't get a signal here.'

'Oh…' As she glanced around, wondering if there was a phone she could borrow, he added lightly, 'And knowing we're marooned together with just one bed, might give him a sleepless night.'

'He wouldn't be worried.' But, remembering his attempts at seduction, she found her colour rising. The intimacy that 'marooned together with just one bed' implied, and thinking a strange man might succeed where he'd failed would make him *furious*.

Watching her companion note that blush, she added hastily, 'Tony's my boss.'

'I see,' Joel said in a way that showed he didn't see at all.

'I—I mean he's not my boyfriend.'

'Well, either way, if he has any sense he won't be expecting you back on a night like this.'

He was no doubt right, Bethany thought, and abandoning any idea of phoning, dropped the mobile back into her bag.

Stretching long legs towards the fire, Joel asked idly, 'What kind of business are you in?'

'Antiques,' she answered quietly, still a little overawed by his presence.

'Your own business?'

She shook her head and her hair, listened in the candlelight. 'No. Tony, my boss, owns Feldon Antiques.'

'Of course,' Joel murmured.

'But I am picking up small, affordable pieces that Feldon Antiques wouldn't touch, with a view to one day starting my own business.'

'You're the buyer?'

She hesitated. Respecting her judgement and knowledge of antiques, a year before his death James had made her the firm's buyer, trusting her to buy at a keen but fair price.

Since Tony had taken over, however, though he relied on her to seek out and identify the rarer items they dealt in—items they sold on to collectors worldwide—he hadn't allowed her to put a price on them.

But she was still the official buyer, she reminded herself, and answered firmly, 'Yes.'

'Does the job involve much travelling?'

'An occasional visit to Europe or the States.'

He raised an eyebrow and questioned, 'So what do you think of The Big Apple?'

'I think New York's wonderful. I remember first falling in love with it when as a young girl I saw *Breakfast at Tiffany's*.' Bethany smiled at the memory.

He grinned. 'And I remember falling in love with Audrey Hepburn.'

For a little while they discussed their favourite old films, then he harked back to query, 'Presumably with your job you put in long hours?'

'Yes, but then I get time off in lieu. This week I'll be in the shop on Wednesday, then I've got until Monday off.'

'What sort of things do you look out for when you're on your travels?'

She thought for a moment then replied, 'Silver and porcelain mainly, but really anything that's rare and valuable.'

'Like this pretty bauble, for instance?' He touched the bracelet she wore, an intricate gold hoop set with deep red stones.

Her heart beating faster, she looked down at his hand, a strong, well-shaped hand with long lean fingers and neatly trimmed nails.

'How did you come by it?' There was a strange note in his voice, an undercurrent of... what? Anger? Condemnation?

But when she looked up the only emotion his face was showing was polite interest, and she knew she must have imagined it.

'Someone brought it into the shop. Though I originally intended it for my collection I loved it on sight, so I decided to keep it.'

'I'm a complete ignoramus when it comes to things like this,' he remarked, turning it round on her wrist. 'I've no real idea how old it is—my guess would be Victorian?'

Only too aware of his touch, she strove to sound cool and unmoved as she told him, 'It dates from the early eighteen hundreds.'

A shade breathlessly, she added, 'Often that kind of bracelet was accompanied by a matching necklace and earrings, which would have made it a lot more valuable. I would have loved a set, but unfortunately it was sold as a single item.'

'May I ask what kind of price a thing like this would fetch?'

She told him what she'd paid for it.

A muscle jumped in his jaw as if he'd clenched his teeth, but his voice was even as he remarked, 'I would have thought—as it's gold and rubies—that it was worth a great deal more than that.'

She shook her head. 'Had it been gold and rubies it would have been, but the stones are garnets.'

'They look like rubies. I always understood that garnets were transparent?' he pursued.

'They are. It's the way these stones are set that makes them look like rubies. Even the seller thought they were.'

'I see.' His expression relaxed.

There was a short silence before he changed the subject by saying, 'I suppose you must meet some interesting people in your line of business?'

Noting how his thick, healthy-looking hair had now dried to its natural ripe-corn colour and longing to touch it, she answered distractedly, 'Yes, you could say that.'

When he waited expectantly, she added, 'The old lady I went to see this morning looked as if she'd stepped out of the pages of some period novel.

'She was dressed all in black, with jet earrings, and was still talking to her husband, who'd been dead for over five years.'

Joel smiled, then, his voice casual, queried, 'She had some antiques she wanted to sell?'

'An attic full,' Bethany said drily.

'Did you find anything worth having?'

She shook her head. She had been hoping to discover something rare and valuable, both for the old lady's sake and—needing to appease Tony's anger—her own. But the 'antiques' had turned out to be, at the best, collectibles, at the worst, junk.

'No valuable silver or porcelain?'

Wondering why he was displaying such interest, she answered, 'The only thing we might have considered buying was a Hochst group of porcelain figures. But unfortunately it had been damaged and mended so badly that it's virtually worthless.'

Leaving his chair to pile more logs on the fire, he remarked, 'So it was a fruitless journey.'

'I'm afraid so.'

In reality it had been anything but. She was with Joel at last and they had the whole of the night in which to get to know one another.

Watching his broad back, noticing how the fine material of his dark sweater stretched across the mature width of his shoulders, she felt a fluttery excitement in her stomach.

The fire blazing to his satisfaction, he gathered up the

crockery and put it on the draining board before washing his hands.

While they talked, almost imperceptibly the light from the lamp had got dimmer, and beyond the glow from the fire shadows were gathering.

Picking up the lamp, Joel moved it from side to side gently. 'I'm afraid we're almost out of oil.'

After a quick search through the cupboards he said, 'There doesn't appear to be any more, so it's a good thing it's almost bedtime.'

He filled the kettle and put it on the stove, remarking, 'It might not be a bad idea to get the bed made up while we can still see what we're doing.'

Recognizing the truth of that, she went to the cupboard and took out bed linen, pillows and a duvet.

Instead of presuming it was woman's work and leaving her to it, as some men would have done, Joel came to help.

The moment she moved away from the fire the cold air had wrapped around her, and she began to feel thoroughly chilled.

As they made the bed together, seeing her shiver, he remarked, 'The duvet appears to be a reasonable weight, so it should be warm enough in bed.'

Suddenly focusing on the fact that there was only the *one* bed, she felt her stomach start to churn.

Picking up her excitement and apparently interpreting it as alarm, he said, 'Don't worry, the bed's all yours.'

In a strangled voice, she queried, 'Well, if I have the bed, where will you sleep?'

'I'll make do with the armchair and a blanket.'

'There aren't any blankets, and only one duvet.'

Sounding anything but worried, he said, 'In that case I'll have to keep the fire well stoked…

'Now, as I estimate that the lamp has only a few minutes' burning time if we're lucky, you'd better have the bathroom first.' Tongue-in-cheek, he added, 'There's soap and towels, but I suppose you don't fancy a cold shower?'

'You suppose right,' she said with feeling.

He grinned. 'A kettle of hot water?'

'Absolute luxury.'

'Not a difficult woman to please.'

'The only thing I mind is not being able to clean my teeth,' she admitted.

Opening the nearest cupboard, he produced two cellophane-wrapped courtesy packs each containing a disposable toothbrush and toothpaste. 'As to all intents and purposes we're hotel guests, I suggest we borrow a couple of these.'

'Wonderful.'

He handed her the packs, then carried the lamp and the kettle through to the bathroom and set them down on a shelf.

'Will you manage at that?'

'Very well, thank you,' she said gratefully.

'Then I'll leave you to it.' He went out, closing the door behind him.

Bethany cleaned her teeth in water so cold it almost made them ache, then slipping off her bracelet, washed in half a kettleful of hot water, leaving Joel the other half.

It was so cold in the bathroom she could see her breath on the air, but just the knowledge that he was close at hand made her feel warm inside. Being together like this, she could almost imagine they were married.

When she had finished, she hastened back to the fire to comb out her long dark hair while he took her place in the bathroom.

When he returned he brought the oil lamp, which was on its last expiring glimmer, and the empty kettle.

'Generous woman,' he remarked, adding, as he refilled the kettle and lit the gas, 'I thought you might like a hot drink before we turn in?'

'I would, please.'

Having washed their two mugs and made coffee, he came to sit beside her again, stretching his long legs towards the hearth.

The lamp flame had finally died, leaving the rest of the room full of shadows and making the circle formed by the flickering fireglow cosy and intimate.

Their coffee finished, she had just taken a breath to ask him about himself when he invited casually, 'Tell me how you got into the antiques business.'

'It was something I'd always wanted to do. Though my father is an accountant, he's always been fascinated by old and beautiful things. A fascination he passed on to me, along with quite a bit of knowledge, so when I left school I got a job with Feldon Antiques in London.'

'London's a big place… and I'm quite sure we've never met. It's just…'

Studying her lovely heart-shaped face in the firelight, the long-lashed grey eyes and dark winged brows, the neat nose and generous mouth, the determined chin that added such character, he went on with a half smile, 'I have the strangest feeling I've seen you somewhere before… You have a face I seem to recognize. To remember…'

When, suddenly transfixed and with her heart racing wildly, she just gazed at him, he went on, 'But perhaps you don't know the feeling of something half-remembered…?'

As she held her breath a log settled with a rustle and a little explosion of bright sparks.

'Maybe it was in my dreams that I met you…' He reached out and ran a fingertip down the curve of her cheek to the little cleft in her chin. 'Maybe in some dream I've kissed your mouth, held you close, made love to you…'

Tracing her lips, he added softly, 'It's what I've wanted to do since the first moment I saw you…'

Caught up in the magic, she sat quite still while her heart swelled and every bone in her body melted.

'It's what I want to do now…' he added softly and, leaning forward, touched his mouth to hers.

His kiss was like no other she had ever experienced before. It held all she'd ever wanted—the delight, the excitement, the warmth and comfort, the sheer joy of belonging.

As her lips parted beneath his, he deepened the kiss until she was on fire with longing, a quivering mass of sensations even before he rose and, lifting her to her feet, drew her against his firm body.

When, still kissing her, he began to run his hands over her, she leaned into him, making soft little noises in her throat.

Even the feel of the cold air on her skin when he removed her clothes and the coolness of the sheets when he lifted her into bed didn't break the spell he'd woven.

And when he slid into bed beside her and drew her against the naked warmth of his body it was like coming home.

He was a good lover, strong, masterful, passionate, yet those qualities went hand in hand with skill and caring, a boundless generosity. Not once but twice he sent her sky-rocketing to the stars with an effortless ease, before gathering her into the crook of his arm and drawing her close.

Snuggled against him, all passion spent, her body sleek and satisfied, her mind euphoric, she knew she had never been so wildly happy, so blissfully content. She was with him at last.

Thinking how wonderful it was that he was under the same kind of spell that she was under, that the enchantment was mutual, she slipped into sleep saying a silent but heartfelt prayer of thanks.

* * *

When Bethany awoke, just for a second or two she was completely disorientated, then memories of the previous night, of Joel, came crowding into her mind filling her with gladness.

Sighing, she reached out to touch him. The space beside her was empty and cold. Pushing herself up on one elbow, she looked around in the semi-darkness.

There was no sign of him and though her clothes still lay where they had been discarded, his had vanished. But, of course, he would be in the bathroom getting washed and dressed.

The fire, though still in, had burnt low and, her naked body goosefleshing, she got out of bed and began to hurriedly pull on her own clothes.

As soon as she was dressed she piled on some logs and went to draw back the curtains. The fog had cleared but the morning was gloomy and overcast with a sky the colour of pewter.

Wondering what time it was, she glanced at her watch. Almost a quarter past nine.

She grimaced. Tony would be livid. He had made it abundantly clear that if they didn't need to stay another day he wanted to make an early start back to the great metropolis.

But even the thought of how furious he would be when she turned up so late and with nothing to show for her visit to Mrs Deramack failed to spoil her new-found happiness.

Though, as yet, she still knew little about Joel except that he came from London, they were together at last. Lovers. In love for ever. A glowing future ahead of them.

While she waited for him to emerge, she put the kettle on, rinsed two mugs and spooned instant coffee into them, before going back to the fire.

Reaching for her capacious bag, she flipped it open and started to unzip the compartment that held her comb and cosmetics.

But something—it looked like the corner of a facial tissue—

was caught and the zip had jammed, though it had seemed all right the previous night when she had replaced her comb.

And her mobile wasn't in the pocket she usually kept it in, but no doubt she had been too excited to care where she put it.

A little frown of concentration marring her smooth brow, she worked the zip free, then, having combed her hair, took it up into its usual gleaming coil.

As she clipped it into place, it began to impinge on her consciousness that, apart from the crackle of burning logs and the kettle starting to sing, everywhere was silent. There wasn't another sound. No movement. No running water. And when she'd put the kettle on it had been cold.

Trying to subdue a sudden, completely unreasonable panic, she went and tapped on the bathroom door. 'Joel… Will you be long?'

There was no answer.

She threw open the door to find the room was empty.

He must have gone across to have a word with the caretaker, she told herself, and, judging by how low the fire had been, he'd been gone for some time, so no doubt he'd be back at any moment.

When another five minutes had passed with no sign of him returning, an icy vice began to tighten around her heart.

But after all they had shared the previous night, he wouldn't have just gone. Walked away without a single word. He *couldn't*.

Of course! All at once the solution struck her. He'd gone to fetch his car. If he had woken her up, she could have driven him there. Though the road had been too narrow at that precise spot for any manoeuvring, there must surely be *somewhere* on that stretch a car could turn round.

When the kettle boiled she made a single cup of coffee and drank it sitting in front of the fire.

After another half an hour had crawled past she knew with

dreadful certainty that he wasn't coming back. Perhaps, subconsciously, she had known from the very beginning.

Joel had gone for good. Had gone without a word. Without so much as leaving a note.

He had walked in and out of her life like some wraith. All she knew about him was his name and the fact that he came from London. He might even be a married man.

Gripped by an icy coldness, a pain so intense she might have been in the grim embrace of an iron maiden, she could neither move nor breathe.

Last night had meant nothing to him. Just a seized chance. A one night stand. All the talk about seeming to know her, to recognize her, had just been part of his seduction technique.

Perhaps he had believed Tony was her lover? Had decided she was easy?

Well, she *had* been, she thought bitterly. Stupidly, idiotically easy.

In love with a dream, she had behaved like some silly little adolescent who hadn't yet learnt to curb her impulses and respect herself.

She stood for a long time staring blindly into space before she was able to move, to find her coat and bag and make her way to the car.

The keys were in the ignition where Joel had left them the previous night. Thinking of how excited she had been when they arrived here, how hopeful, she felt as if a knife was being turned in her heart and was forced to lean against the car until the worst of the agony had passed.

Then, her usual graceful movements clumsy, she got into the driving seat and, leaning forward, rested her forehead on the wheel.

After a moment or two, as if so much pain had caused a protective shield to drop into place, she raised her head and, neither

thinking nor feeling, her entire being numb, drove back to
Dundale like some automaton.

It was almost twelve by the time she reached the Inn to find
Tony pacing the lobby, every bit as enraged as she had imagined.

'So here you are at last! I wondered what the devil had
happened to you. Have you any idea how long I've been waiting?' he demanded angrily.

Her voice curiously flat and lifeless, she said, 'I'm sorry. I'm
afraid I overslept.'

'Overslept!' He uttered a profanity. 'So where the hell did
you sleep?'

Briefly, she explained about the burst tyre and the mist and
having to spend the night at a hotel that was still officially closed
for the winter. She didn't mention Joel.

'Why didn't you let me know?' Tony sounded even more ex-
asperated.

'I couldn't get a signal,' she said shortly, and was pleased
when he grunted and left it at that.

'So how did you get on with old Mrs Deramack? Any good
stuff?'

She shook her head.

He swore briefly.

Making an effort at normality, she asked, 'How about
Greendales? They seemed to have some extremely nice things.'

'They did,' he admitted grudgingly, 'but their reserve prices
were a damn sight too high. Private sales make a lot more sense...'

Bethany was aware that, translated, that meant *a lot more
money*. James Feldon had cared about antiques. All Tony cared
about was the bottom line.

'That's why I was hoping the old lady had something worth
our while. As it is, the trip's been a waste of time. And now

you've managed to sleep in,' he added nastily, 'it's been a waste of a morning too.'

'I'm sorry,' she said again.

'I hope you weren't expecting to have lunch before we start?'

'No, I'm not at all hungry. I'll just fetch my things.' She couldn't wait to get away.

Except for a short stop to refuel and have coffee and, in Tony's case, a packet of sandwiches, they drove straight back to town. Still in a foul mood, apart from occasionally cursing another motorist, Tony barely uttered a word.

It was a relief in one way, but it allowed too much time for brooding. The numbness had passed and, her thoughts bleak as winter, Bethany found herself going over and over everything that had happened the previous night. Picking at it. Dissecting it. Exposing the pain, so that it was like doing an autopsy on a living body.

By the time Tony dropped her at her flat she was feeling like death and only too pleased that Catherine, who was an airline stewardess, was away until the following week and she had the place to herself.

Quite unable to stomach the thought of food, even though she'd had nothing to eat that day, Bethany made herself a pot of tea and sat down to drink it. She would have an early night. She needed the blessed oblivion of sleep.

Tomorrow, though her beautiful dreams had turned to dust, she would have to get up and face the day as if nothing had happened. If that were possible.

But it *had* to be. She must *make* it possible.

She recalled a motto in one of last year's Christmas crackers: *When your dreams turn to dust, Hoover.* It seemed appropriate.

Her tea finished, she was heading for the bedroom when the phone rang.

For a moment she considered not answering. But old habits died hard and, before she could make herself walk away, she had picked up the receiver.

'Hello?'

'So you're back…'

It was Michael Sharman. Over the last few months she had got to know and like him and they had been out together on quite a number of occasions but she saw him as nothing more than a friend.

'Bethany?'

She wasn't in the mood to talk to anybody. She sighed, 'Yes, I'm back.'

'It doesn't sound like you.'

'I'm a bit tired.'

He went on regardless, seemingly oblivious to her overwhelming tiredness. 'I tried to phone you earlier. Been home long?'

'No.'

'Care to go out for a spot of supper?'

'I don't think so, Michael.' She wasn't in the right kind of mood to go out.

'Why not?' he asked.

'I was just on my way to bed.'

'Bed?' he exclaimed, surprised. 'But it's barely eight o'clock. Look, what if I pop round now and pick you up?'

'No, thank you. I'm tired.' Then, aware that she'd sounded a bit curt, she added apologetically, 'I'm sorry. I guess I'm even more tired than I thought.'

'Sure I can't change your mind? Going out might be just what you need to liven you up.'

'I doubt it.'

He was a young man who was used to getting his own way with women. But this woman was special, not like the rest, and he didn't want to spoil his chances.

'In that case,' he said reluctantly, 'let's make it tomorrow night.'

'Well, I—'

'What if I pick you up around seven? We'll go to the Caribbean Club and have a good time.'

Before she could argue, he was gone.

Sighing, she replaced the receiver.

If she found she couldn't face it, she would just have to call him and put him off.

But what would she do if she did stay at home? What was she *likely* to do?

Mope. Which would get her precisely nowhere.

Going out with Michael had to be preferable.

After first thinking him somewhat cocky and immature, she had come to enjoy his company and almost envy his carefree, sybaritic attitude to life.

They had first met when, after inheriting his grandmother's house and its contents, he had brought a blue and white porcelain bowl into Feldon Antiques, saying he needed to raise some ready cash.

Bethany, who had been in the shop at the time, had thought the bowl was Ming, which would have made it extremely valuable. But an expert on Chinese porcelain that Tony had later taken it to had identified it as Qing, which made its value a great deal less.

However, it was still worth a considerable amount and Michael had been more than happy to part with it.

After selling them the bowl, he had produced several smaller items which Tony had dismissed but Bethany had been pleased to buy for her collection.

The bracelet Joel had admired had been one of them.

But where was the bracelet?

A moment's thought convinced her that she had taken it off

in the bathroom the previous night before getting washed. She hadn't noticed it that morning, nor had she given it a thought, but she had had other things on her mind.

Just to be on the safe side, she found her shoulder bag and searched through it, but there was no sign of the bracelet in its capacious depths.

She must have left it at the hotel.

It was a blow, even though she hadn't really *expected* to find it—looking in her bag had been an act of sheer desperation.

If it were possible, her spirits sank even lower. Until then, despite all the pain, she hadn't shed a single tear, but, as though leaving her bracelet was the last straw, she began to cry.

She cried until she had no more tears left, then, feeling empty, drained, hollow as a ghost, showered and crawled into bed.

In the morning she would have to try and get in touch with the caretaker...

Following closely on that thought came a sense of helplessness. She didn't even know the name of the hotel they had stayed at. All she knew was that it lay at the foot of Dunscar.

But if she contacted the nearest information centre, supposing there was one open in early February, they should be able to give her the name of the place...

After a night spent tossing and turning, Bethany got up feeling heavy-eyed and heavy-hearted. Though she had no appetite, before setting off for the shop, she made herself eat some breakfast—a triumph of common sense over despair.

It was a bleak, grey morning that perfectly matched her mood. The only bright spot was when Tony, still noticeably surly, announced that when he'd dealt with the morning's mail he was going out and would be gone for the rest of the day.

After working several weekends in a row, she was entitled to three days off, which meant she wouldn't have to come in again until Monday, and, as things were, she could only be glad.

In their absence, her colleague Alison had been her usual efficient self and there was no backlog of work.

With nothing pressing to do, Bethany set out to find the name of the hotel at the foot of Dunscar. The area's central information bureau was open and able to tell her that it was called The Dunbeck. They even provided the phone number.

Somewhat heartened, she dialled the number.

There was no answer.

Though she tried periodically for the rest of the day, she met with no success.

Just as she was about to close the shop a couple of browsers came in and it was turned six before she was able to lock up and leave.

By the time she reached her basement flat, tired and frustrated, it was almost six-thirty and Michael would be picking her up at seven.

CHAPTER THREE

FEELING anything but sociable, Bethany was tempted to ring and put Michael off, but better sense prevailed. It would do her a lot more good to go out than sit at home brooding.

Her decision made, she drew the curtains against the dark, frosty night and went into the bathroom to have a quick shower.

Dried and scented, she touched a mascara wand to her long lashes and glossed her lips with pale, shiny lipstick. Then, as though making up for her previous lack of enthusiasm, she donned her best dark blue cocktail dress and fastened pearl studs to her small, neat lobes.

Leaving her hair falling loosely around her shoulders in a dark silky cloud, she was ready when the bell rang.

She opened the door to find Michael was waiting beneath the lantern, a bouquet of crimson roses in his hand.

'Wow!' he exclaimed at the sight of her. 'You look fantastic!' Then, handing her the flowers, 'I hope you like roses?'

'Thank you, I do. They're lovely. If you come in for a minute I'll put them in water.'

Following her inside, he leaned against the kitchen counter while she stripped off the cellophane and found a vase to arrange the roses in.

Slimly built and a couple of inches taller than herself, he was well-dressed and well-groomed, a personable young man with dark curly hair and more than his fair share of charm.

From a wealthy background and with a private income, he was, she supposed, quite a catch.

Watching her arrange the flowers, he queried, 'Was it a successful trip?'

She shook her head. 'Not very.'

'I thought you seemed depressed. Oh, well, let's forget our troubles and go and have a good time.'

Wondering what troubles he had in what she had hitherto regarded as a carefree life, she locked the door behind her and followed him up the basement steps to his red Porsche.

During an evening spent dancing and dining at the Caribbean Club, Bethany did her best to hide her misery and appear cheerful. But, despite all her efforts, Michael picked up her low spirits.

When they returned to their table after a slow foxtrot, he remarked sympathetically, 'You really *are* down, aren't you?'

Feeling guilty, she said, 'I'm sorry if I've spoilt your evening.'

He shook his head. 'Of course you haven't spoilt it.' Then, with a sigh, 'I wasn't exactly ecstatic to start with.'

'You have a problem?'

'Too true… I'm in a mess. I need a substantial sum of money and I need it fast.'

Catching her look of surprise, he said, 'If you're thinking of what I got for the bowl… I invested it in a new stage show that was looking for backers.

'If it comes off, it should make everyone involved, me included, multi-millionaires.

'But there's still months to go before it's due to open, and I learnt today that they're running out of cash.'

He sounded so despondent that Bethany's heart went out to him.

'Can't they find extra backers?'

'They've tried, but once it gets around that a project is rocky, no one wants to take that risk. So one way or another, I've just got to come up with some more cash.'

'What about your grandmother's house?'

'Unfortunately I can't sell that.'

'You're fond of it because it was the family home?'

'God, no! Now all the staff are gone, apart from a cleaning lady, it puts me in mind of a mausoleum. I was rattling round the blasted place like a grain of rice in an empty tin until my stepbrother suggested I could move in with him for a while…'

'So you're living with your stepbrother?'

Michael shook his head. 'It didn't work. All he wanted to do was keep an eye on me. He started to tick me off about the hours I kept, so I'm bunking with a mate of mine in a very small flat.'

Gloomily, he added, 'I was hoping to rent a place of my own but my allowance won't stretch to it.'

Then, with a sudden flare of temper, 'I could afford to *buy* a flat and still have a tidy bit left if I was able to put the blasted house on the market.'

Seeing her puzzled frown, he went on, 'But even when things are through probate, thanks to the terms of the will, I can't sell it before I reach the age of twenty-five. That's in two years' time. Until then my stepbrother has control.'

'Couldn't your family help out in the meantime?'

'He's the only family I have left.'

'What does he do?'

'He's an entrepreneur,' Michael said sourly. 'As well as owning JSM International, he has a finger in a great many different pies.'

'So he's a lot older than you?'

'Only six years.'

Seeing her surprise, Michael explained. 'He made his pile young by buying up failing businesses, putting them on their feet again and selling them at a hell of a profit.'

'Well, surely he'd help if you asked him?'

Michael's laugh was bitter. 'You have to be joking! The last time I was forced to ask him for extra cash, he grudgingly paid off my debts. But when I asked him for a bigger allowance, he said it was high time I got a job.

'I pointed out I hadn't been trained for anything.' Miael sighed and went on, 'He offered me a position in his Los Angeles branch. I'm sure the climate would be great, but who in his right senses wants to be tied to an office five days out of seven?

'My only hope is that amongst the rest of my grandmother's antiques there's something really valuable... I suppose you wouldn't be prepared to take a quick look and advise me?'

'Of course. When would you—?'

'Tonight,' he broke in eagerly. 'We can call in there on the way back to your flat...'

Bethany's heart sank. Tired and headachy, it was the last thing she wanted to do, but feeling she owed it to him, she agreed, 'All right.'

Having signalled the waiter, he paid the bill, collected their coats and hurried her out to the waiting car.

In spite of the traffic, in a matter of minutes they were drawing up outside his grandmother's elegant porticoed townhouse in Lanervic Square.

Michael let them in and, closing the door behind them, switched off the alarm.

As he led the way across the spacious hall to a vast and silent living room, Bethany began to realize why he had described the place as a mausoleum.

At first glance all the furniture appeared to be antique, and there were several glass-fronted display cabinets crowded with Chinese pottery and porcelain.

Staggered by the sheer amount of stuff, she stared at it in silence.

After a minute or so, Michael asked eagerly, 'Do you think there'll be something I can raise a good amount on?'

'Almost certainly. How many pieces do you want to part with?'

'One… Two, at the most. Otherwise it might be—' He broke off abruptly.

'Examining even a few pieces is going to take time and care,' Bethany said, 'so it would make more sense to come back tomorrow.'

He took her hand. 'I've a much better idea… Why don't you stay the night?'

Before she could refuse, he had pulled her close and was kissing her with an ardour that just for a second or two swamped her, then she tried to draw away. But his arms were wrapped tightly around her and he was so much stronger than she had imagined.

She was gathering herself to struggle in earnest, when all at once she was free and Michael, his startled face an unbecoming brick-red, was goggling at something behind her.

Turning to follow the direction of his gaze, she saw that there was a tall fair-haired man with wide shoulders lounging in the doorway.

Feeling as if she'd walked slap into a plate glass window, she found herself staring at Joel.

Michael was the first to break the silence with a stammered, 'H-hell… you startled me.'

'So I see,' Joel said smoothly.

With a hint of bravado, Michael asked, 'What are you doing here?'

'I could ask you the same question.' A bite to his tone, Joel added, 'Only the answer seems obvious. Unless I have the wrong end of the stick?'

All the colour draining from his face, Michael stammered, 'Well I—I just brought Bethany in to… to… see where I used to live.'

Joel glanced at her as if he'd never met her before in his life and, his little smile contemptuous, drawled, 'Really?'

'There's nothing wrong with that, is there?' Michael blustered. 'In any case we were just on the point of leaving.'

'Then I'll say goodnight to you both.'

Throughout the little exchange, shocked and stunned, incapable of coherent thought, Bethany had stood there, transfixed, her wide eyes on Joel's face.

Now she found herself hurried out of the house and across the pavement to the red Porsche as if the hounds of hell were baying at their heels.

'That's blown it!' Michael exclaimed as he slid behind the wheel and started the car. 'He must have overheard everything. What rotten luck for him to walk in just at that minute.'

While Bethany was still fumbling to fasten her seatbelt, they set off with a whoosh that threw her back in her seat.

'Was that…?' Her voice failed. She swallowed hard and tried again. 'Was that your stepbrother?'

'Yes, for my sins. And now you see what I mean?' he went on as he joined the traffic stream. 'See what a swine he is?

'He's always been an arrogant bastard, but now he holds the purse-strings he thinks he rules the world and other places.

'Well, at the moment he might have the whip hand. But one of these days I'll be my own master. I won't have to kowtow to him any longer…'

During the silence that followed, Bethany made an attempt to gather herself and come to terms with the almost unbelievable.

It seemed so strange, so bizarre, that Joel was Michael's step-brother. She felt as if fate was playing the jester. Mocking her. Making fun of her. Having a game at her expense.

Meeting him again out of the blue like that had shaken her to the core. But what had disturbed her even more was the way he had looked at her. As if she'd crawled from under a stone. As if he held her in contempt.

Obviously he had heard Michael asking her to stay the night and presumed they were already lovers. After what had happened in the Lakes, he must have thought her immoral. A woman who had no principles, who would sleep with a man she knew nothing about, a man she had only just met.

If he'd respected her at all, he wouldn't have left the next morning without a single word.

It was the old double standard. Yet somehow it still held sway.

Her unhappy thoughts were interrupted when the car drew up outside her flat.

Michael got out and accompanied her across the pavement. When she paused at the top of the area steps, he asked, 'Can I come in?'

It was the last thing she wanted. She felt much too churned up. Too agitated.

She was about to make some excuse when he added, 'God, do I need a brandy!'

As a rule, when he was driving he made a point of not drinking but, glancing at his face in the glow from the street lamp, she could see that he really did need something to steady him.

Turning, she led the way down the steps and unlocked the door. He followed her into the cosy warmth and threw himself into one of the comfortable linen-covered armchairs while she took off her coat.

Finding a glass, she poured a measure of brandy from a bottle Devlin had brought for some party or other and handed it to him.

'Thanks.' He downed it in a single gulp and held out his glass for more.

'You're driving,' she reminded him.

'Just a small one,' he coaxed.

Putting the bottle back in the cupboard, she said firmly, 'I'll make some coffee.'

'You're acting like a wife,' he accused.

Ignoring that, she said, 'You don't want to risk losing your licence, do you?'

'God, no!'

While he stared moodily into space she made a pot of good strong coffee and handed him a cup, before sitting on the couch.

He took a sip, then, putting the cup down so that it rattled in the saucer, asked abruptly, 'Suppose we get married?'

'Married?' she echoed blankly.

'Why not? You know I'm mad about you. You've got everything I've been looking for in a woman. We could have a lot of fun together.'

She shook her head emphatically. 'The whole idea is ridiculous.'

'What's so ridiculous about it?' He sounded hurt. 'I may not have much money at the moment, but I *will* have plenty. I don't have to work for a living. I have a top-of-the-range car...'

It occurred to her to wonder how, if his allowance was 'a mere pittance' as he'd claimed, he could afford to own and run a car like that.

But he was going on. 'The family I belong to is an influential one, and you'd have a place in society.'

Thinking about Joel, she said, 'I'm sorry, Michael, it's out of the question.'

'Why is it out of the question?'

Agitation brought her to her feet. 'W-well for one thing, I don't love you.'

'Give it time and you might change your mind.'

'I'm sorry, Michael, it just wouldn't work.'

He got up and, taking her shoulders, said seriously, 'Look, don't say anything now. Sleep on it.' With an attempt at a grin, he added, 'Perhaps by morning the idea will seem a little more appealing...

'Tell you what, have lunch with me and give me your answer then.' Snatching a quick kiss, he let himself out.

She sank back on the couch, her mind a confused jumble of thoughts. Before she could begin to sort out that confusion, she heard his footsteps returning and his knock at the door.

Glancing around to see what he'd left, she went to open it. As soon as the latch was off, the door was held to prevent her shutting it again and a man that *wasn't* Michael brushed past her. Closing the door behind him, he set his back to the panels.

Both her heart and breathing seemed to stop as, for the second time that night, she found herself staring at Joel.

Then, her heart starting to race wildly, she stammered, 'W-what are you doing here? How did you know where I lived?'

'I followed you home,' he admitted shamelessly.

'What do you want?'

'I want to talk to you.' His voice was as cool as his silvery-green eyes.

When she continued to stand gaping at him, he said, 'I presume we're alone?'

Making a great effort to pull herself together, she said, 'Yes.'

'Good. Suppose we sit down?'

Bethany forced her shaky legs to carry her across to the couch once more.

Joel waited politely until she was sitting down before removing his short car-coat and taking the chair opposite.

Wearing casual trousers and a black polo-necked sweater that made his hair seem even fairer, he looked dangerously attractive.

His mere presence overwhelmed her but, not wanting him to gain the upper hand, she took a deep breath and asked as steadily as possible, 'What do you want to talk about?'

His eyes fixed on her face, he said, 'Knowing Michael, I strongly suspect he's going to ask you to marry him…'

Then, reading her expression correctly, 'Ah, I see he's already asked you. I hope you haven't accepted.'

Ruffled by the casual arrogance of his manner, she looked him in the eye and said shortly, 'That has nothing to do with you.'

He laughed mockingly. 'That's just where you're wrong. It has *everything* to do with me. *What answer did you give him?*'

Her eyes fell beneath his and she shook her head.

'I haven't given him a final answer yet.'

'Good.' Joel's voice held satisfaction. 'When is he expecting one?'

'Tomorrow, when he picks me up for lunch,' Bethany said quietly.

He looked her directly in the eye. 'You'll say no, of course.'

It was an order.

Refusing to be intimidated further, she lied, 'I haven't made up my mind yet.'

His tone became angry. 'Well, get this into your pretty little head, there's no way I'll allow you to marry him.'

'You might have some financial control over Michael's life,' she said furiously, 'but you can't stop him marrying whoever he wants to marry. And you certainly can't tell *me* what to do.'

There was silence for a second or two, then Joel spoke.

'That's quite true. If you're determined to marry him, I can't stop you. All the same, it would be a sad mistake.'

'Why are you so against it?' she asked without stopping to think.

He raised a level brow.

Flushing, she supplied her own answer. 'Because you think I have no morals.'

'Now, why should I think that?' he asked mockingly.

'Because…' She stopped, her colour rising.

'Because you've slept with both of us?'

'That's not so.'

'Don't tell me that holding you in my arms, feeling your naked body against mine, making love to you, was just a dream!' he said with a smirk.

Hating the derision in his voice, she said thickly, 'I haven't slept with Michael.'

'Never?'

'Never.'

Joel raised an eyebrow, as if questioning her response. 'I heard him invite you to stay the night.'

'If he hadn't kissed me when he did, you would have heard me refuse.'

'Playing hard to get? Or would *Tony* have objected?'

Bethany was furious. 'Tony is my boss, not my boyfriend.'

'That's what you said before.'

'But you don't believe me.'

'I might have done if, at the Dundale Inn, you hadn't been booked in as Mr and Mrs Feldon.'

Taken aback, she demanded, 'How do you know that?'

He answered her question with a question of his own. 'It's the truth, isn't it?'

Taking a deep breath, she said, 'Yes, but Tony had made the booking without my knowledge…'

It was quite obvious that Joel didn't believe her. Even so, she ploughed on. 'He was hoping to "have a little fun" as he put it—'

'So presumably he's used to *having a little fun*.'

Bethany lifted her chin. 'Not with *me*, he isn't. I don't even like him. But since I broke my engagement he's been trying to get me to go to—'

'Who were you engaged to?'

She saw by his face that she was digging herself in deeper. 'His name was Devlin.'

'Why did you break it off?'

'I came back from a business trip to find him in bed with another woman.'

When she said no more, Joel prompted, 'So your boss has been trying to get you to "have a little fun" but so far he hasn't succeeded…'

Bethany crossed her arms in a gesture of defiance. 'No, he hasn't.'

Joel smiled wryly, and she knew so exactly what he was thinking—*yet you let a perfect stranger seduce you*—that he might have spoken the words aloud.

She bit her lip.

'To have booked a double room he must have been fairly confident,' Joel pursued.

'His confidence was misplaced,' she said shortly. 'When I discovered what he'd done, I insisted on having a separate room.'

'Really?' he drawled.

'Yes, really. If you'd checked further you would have found that I slept in number nine. On my own,' she added for good measure.

'That couldn't have pleased our Lothario.'

'No, it didn't. He called me prim and proper.'

With a sardonic gleam in his eye, Joel remarked, 'I certainly wouldn't call you prim and proper. Quite the opposite, in fact… But do go on.'

Feeling her face grow hot, she added hardily, 'I told him I didn't sleep around and—'

Joel gave a little bark of laughter. 'I suppose it depends on what you mean by "sleep around".'

She felt the prick of angry tears and was forced to blink. 'You think I'm easy, don't you? That's why you don't want me to marry Michael.'

'I don't want you to marry Michael for a variety of reasons,' he informed her coolly.

'Such as?'

His mouth a little wry, he admitted, 'Perhaps I'm jealous. Perhaps I want you for myself.'

Hardly daring to believe it, she stared at him in silence, the breath caught in her throat.

Rising, he took her hand and pulled her to her feet. Bethany was tall, but at over six feet he had a good five inches on her.

Looming over her, he looked at her with a quiet intensity that made heat spread through her entire body. Then, with deliberation, he brushed the pad of his thumb across her lips.

As she read the intent, the purpose, in his face, a shiver ran through her. The hammer blows of her heart threatening to break her ribs, she backed away a step or two until she stopped by the wall, whispering, 'Don't. Please don't.'

'Don't what?' he asked, closing in on her.

'Kiss me,' she said desperately. 'I don't want you to kiss me.'

He put a hand each side of her head, trapping her there. 'But of course I'm going to kiss you. You know perfectly well you want me to.'

His voice soft and seductive as silk, he went on, 'And I've been thinking of nothing else since I last saw you.'

He took her heart-shaped face between his hands to hold her head still while he kissed her, teasing first with his tongue, then nipping gently at her bottom lip.

At first she made an effort to keep her lips pressed tightly together, but after a few moments, unable to help herself, they parted beneath that skilful coaxing.

With a little murmur of male satisfaction, he took instant advantage.

His kiss was long and lazy, yet with a leashed hunger that scattered her wits and swamped any attempt at rational thought.

After a while he lifted his head and looked into her face. Her eyes were closed, long lashes making dark fans on her cheeks, her lips dewy, a flush of colour lying along her high cheekbones.

Almost wonderingly, he murmured, 'You're quite exquisite. You have the kind of beauty that men often dream about but are seldom lucky enough to find...'

Pleasure running through her that he thought her beautiful, it barely registered when he added almost to himself, 'If the inside matched, you'd be one of the most perfect things nature ever created...'

Sliding one hand beneath the silky fall of dark hair, he cupped her nape and drew her head forward until his mouth had captured hers again.

Exploring, tantalizing, dominating, by turns, his kisses sent shivers of delight and excitement coursing up and down her spine.

While he kissed her, he moved his hands caressingly over her slender curves, tracing her hips and buttocks, her waist and ribcage and the soft swell of her breasts.

He brushed a nipple lightly and, feeling her shudder, whispered into her mouth, 'I want to take you to bed and strip you naked, to pleasure you until you're a quivering mass of sensations in my hands. I want to feel your body against mine, to make love to you until you're mindless. Then I want to do it all over again…'

Somewhere, buried deep, the still, small voice of common sense warned that she should send him away. If she let him make love to her now, after the way he'd walked out on her, it would only reinforce his belief that she was easy.

But, even as she tried to hold on to that thought, she could feel it slipping away, feel her resolve weakening as his mouth moved against hers and his hands brought every nerve ending in her body zinging into life.

Though she knew virtually nothing about him, she knew with absolute certainty that out of all the men in the world *this* man was the one she had been waiting for, the other part of her, the part that finally made her whole. He was her love, her destiny.

Though it sounded like a sentiment from some romantic movie, it didn't make it any less true.

When he stooped and, one arm beneath her knees, the other supporting her shoulders, lifted her high in his arms, on fire for him, she made no protest.

Her bedroom door was ajar and, having shouldered it open, he carried her inside and, setting her down carefully, switched on the lamp. Then, slipping off her shoes and dress and slip, he led her over to the bed and laid her on it, before swiftly stripping off his own clothes and sitting down beside her.

The last time he had removed her clothes it had been almost dark and cold enough to make her skin goose-flesh even though he'd been fast and deft.

This time it was comfortably warm and, the glow from the bedside lamp gilding the smooth creaminess of her flawless skin, he undressed her slowly, savouring each moment.

First he unhooked her bra and tossed it aside, pausing to admire her firm, beautifully shaped breasts with their dusky pink nipples.

Next came her silk stockings—one of her few extravagances—which he rolled down her long slender legs slowly, erotically, pausing to massage first one foot and then the other, kneading and stroking, working between her toes, finding previously unknown pressure points.

The feelings he engendered were amazing, each toe sensitive to his touch, each one turning into an erogenous zone, making her nipples firm and her stomach clench.

By the time he removed her lacy panties, she was eager to feel his weight. But, clearly in no hurry, though he was obviously aroused, he moved his attention to her shoulders, stroking and caressing, following the line of her collarbone to the hollow at the base of her throat.

Having lingered there as though reluctant to leave, his fingertips went on to trace the curve of her breasts and the warm cleft between them.

As his mouth took the place of his fingers, a slight stubble accentuating the sensations, she quivered with anticipation. But, as though determined to tease, while he explored the soft firmness with his tongue and lips, occasionally nibbling gently, he avoided her nipples.

She was in an agony of suspense before he began to lave first one and then the other, causing spasms of pleasure to run through her. When his mouth finally closed over one dusky peak, sucking and tugging slightly, and his fingers teased the other, the sensations were so exquisite that she began to gasp and squirm.

Wondering dimly how he could hold back for so long and eager to feel his body against hers, eager for his possession, she moved her hips with an instinctive invitation as old as Eve.

Lifting his head, he smiled and, and as though in answer to her question, told her, 'The more the sensations build, the more intense and prolonged it makes the pleasure for both of us…'

One hand following her ribcage down to her flat stomach and past the nest of dark silky curls to the moist, silken warmth of her inner thighs, he murmured, 'But I think we're almost there…'

For a moment or two he inched her closer to the brink and she was almost mindless when he finally lowered himself into the cradle of her hips.

Unable to help herself, she cried out as his first strong thrust sent her tumbling and spinning into the abyss of pleasure.

It took a long time to fall and she was still quivering with ecstasy as she heard his groan and felt the weight of his head heavy on her breast.

When the heated bliss changed to a glowing warmth and their heartbeats and breathing returned to something like normal, he drew away, leaving her momentarily cold and alone. Then, having switched out the light, he gathered her against him and settled her head on his shoulder.

Once more all was right with the world and within moments she was asleep.

After a while he awoke her with a kiss.

Her heart overflowing with love and gratitude that miraculously everything had come right, she nestled against him and returned his kiss.

This time their love-making was just as intense, but different. He moved with maddening slowness, withdrawing to the very tip then pressing back again, sending shuddering thrills through her.

Then, as she abandoned herself to the slowly spiralling bliss, the rhythm grew faster and he drove deeper until, her fingers knotted in his hair, her back arched, the night exploded like a rocket into a thousand bright sparks and she cried out at the intensity of the shared pleasure.

For a while she lay blind and transfixed, her fingers unconsciously stroking his hair, savouring his weight and the glorious waves of release surging through her body.

She wanted to cling to this moment, to make it last for ever, but almost before he lifted himself away she had drifted into a blissful sleep.

CHAPTER FOUR

WHEN Bethany awoke it was to a singing happiness. The instant awareness that Joel was back in her life. The precious knowledge that, in spite of everything, he still wanted her.

She turned to him in the dimness, only to find that once again the space beside her was cold and empty. Her heart lurched sickeningly. Even as she tried to reassure herself that he would be in the bathroom, something in the quality of the silence convinced her she was alone in the flat.

Pushing herself upright, she glanced around. Sure enough, his clothes were gone.

But that needn't necessarily mean he had walked out on her for a second time. The bedside clock showed it was almost nine forty-five. Perhaps he'd had to go because he had pressing commitments.

But, if that was so, why hadn't he at least told her he was going?

He might not have wanted to wake her.

Oh, stop clutching at straws! she told herself angrily. He had gone because, apart from taking her to bed when the opportunity arose, he had absolutely no interest in her. She was less than nothing to him.

She felt a return of the numbing despair she had felt previously. Maybe he had only made love to her so he could tell

Michael, make it clear to the younger man exactly what kind of woman she was?

Perhaps if she had told him the truth, that she hadn't the faintest intention of marrying his stepbrother, he wouldn't have made such a determined attempt to seduce her.

And it had been determined. But if she had held out against him, refused to allow herself to be seduced a second time, would he have thought any better of her?

Possibly not.

But she would have thought better of herself.

As it was, having made the same mistake twice, she would just have to live with it. Try to forget about Joel, put the whole sorry mess behind her and carry on as best she could.

All she wanted to do at the moment was hide away with her misery, but in less than two hours Michael would be calling for her.

She would have to phone him, she thought in a sudden panic, tell him she was ill…

But that was chickening out. Or, at the best, only a temporary solution. Michael was a persistent young man who wouldn't be easily deterred, so what she *must* do was talk to him face to face and make it clear that they had no future together.

Getting out of bed, she headed for the bathroom, feeling cold and lifeless inside, her limbs as heavy as her spirits.

A hot shower, while it warmed her flesh, did little to dispel that inner coldness and she huddled into a towelling robe as she cleaned her teeth.

When she was dressed in a suit the colour of mulberries and a cream shirt, she coiled her hair and stood before the mirror to pin it into place.

With a flawless skin and dark brows and lashes, she normally needed very little in the way of make-up. But now the sight of herself looking like a ghost, with a pale face and hollow cheeks, had her reaching for her cosmetic case.

She had just finished applying a dab of foundation, a little blusher and a touch of lip-gloss when, without warning, the bedroom door opened.

With a gasp, she spun round.

Joel stood in the doorway looking handsome and relaxed and entirely at home. 'Sorry,' he said easily. 'Did I startle you?'

After a moment of stunned disbelief, life and warmth flowed back in a rush. 'I—I thought you'd gone,' she stammered.

'Because I had things to do, arrangements to make, I left quite early. It seemed a shame to wake you, so I borrowed a key to get back in again if you happened to be still asleep.

'I've been rather longer than I'd anticipated, so I'm glad to see you're dressed and ready. All you need to do is pack a case.'

'Pack a case?' she echoed blankly. 'Why do I need to pack a case?'

Sounding as if he was talking to a not-very-bright child, he told her, 'Because you're spending a long weekend with me.'

As she gaped at him, he urged, 'You want to, don't you?' Though it was phrased as a question, he seemed very sure of her answer.

Knowing that if she meekly agreed he might think the worst of her, she shook her head. 'I—I can't.'

'Why not? The other night you told me you had some days due to you.'

'Yes, I do, but I—'

'Then let's get moving. I'll explain everything later. Where do you keep your travel case?'

Excitement running madly through her veins, she said, 'In that cupboard.'

Almost before the words were out, he had opened the cupboard door and taken out one of her small cases. Tossing it on to the bed, he said, 'Throw anything you might need into that. Oh, and don't forget to pick up your passport.'

Always neat and organized, she swiftly found and packed undies, a nightdress and negligée, a couple of changes of clothing, a simple black cocktail dress and a few accessories.

Looking extremely elegant in well-cut trousers and a soft leather jacket, he leaned against the door jamb, one ankle crossed lazily over the other, and watched her.

Having closed the case and zipped it up, she gathered up her coat and shoulder bag and announced breathlessly, 'I'm ready.'

He straightened, saying approvingly. 'An efficient, focused woman, I see.'

As he picked up her case and began to shepherd her towards the door, suddenly remembering, she blurted out, 'Oh, Michael is expecting me to be here.'

'You can phone him as we go.'

One hand at her waist, Joel hurried her out of the house and up the area steps.

By the kerb, a sleek silver limousine was waiting, a shaft of cold winter sunshine that had pierced the low cloud glancing off its polished bonnet.

As they crossed the pavement a uniformed chauffeur jumped smartly out and held open the passenger door.

As soon as she was installed, Joel handed the chauffeur her case and said, 'Let's hope the traffic's not too bad. Time's tight. If we get delayed we may miss our slot.'

Sliding in beside Bethany, he reached to fasten both their seat belts and a moment later they were on their way.

She had just got her breath back and was about to ask him where they were going, when his mobile rang.

With a murmured, 'Excuse me,' he took it from his pocket and answered briskly, 'Joel McAlister.'

The call was a lengthy one and when it was over he said, 'Sorry about that.'

Dropping the phone back in his pocket, he went on, 'I don't usually let business intrude on my private life, but there's an important deal going through that I've really needed to nurse.

'As I had to be on the spot in person in case anything went wrong, and I wanted to spend these few days with you, I decided it would be admissible, for once, to mix business with pleasure.

'However, everything is going smoothly. Which means I can focus entirely on you.' He smiled into her eyes.

His look was so direct, so intent, it was more like being kissed than looked at. It made her head swim.

He moved a fraction and without conscious volition her eyes closed and her lips parted in anticipation of his kiss.

When it didn't come, flustered, she opened her eyes to find he was still looking at her, an amused, faintly mocking smile hanging on his lips.

As the colour rose in her cheeks, he said softly in her ear, 'If I gave way to the temptation to kiss you I might lose control and I don't want to shock Greaves. He's a pillar of the church and a happily married man.'

Knowing he was making fun of her, she blushed even harder and, turning her head away, stared resolutely out of the car window.

Was she doing the right thing throwing caution to the wind and going off like this with a man she still scarcely knew?

But what was the point of asking herself that? Though she was taking a big risk, though she knew full well it could all end in tears, she had chosen to be with the man she knew she loved.

Or perhaps she'd had no choice? Maybe she was so under his spell that she couldn't help herself?

The thought was an uncomfortable one, and a shiver ran down her spine.

'Cold?' he asked solicitously.

'No… No, not at all…' She smiled weakly.

'If you're sure,' he murmured.

Realizing she'd sounded as uptight as she felt, she made a conscious effort to relax, observing, 'I still don't know where we're going.'

'New York.'

'New York!' Surprise made her jaw drop. If she'd had to hazard a guess it would have been Paris or Amsterdam. 'Why New York?'

'My mother was from New York, and most of my business interests are Anglo-American, so now it's my second home. I thought you might like the idea.'

'Oh, I do… It just seems a long way to go for a weekend, and the flights can be awkward—'

'I have a private jet standing by,' he broke in smoothly, 'which greatly facilitates matters.'

Well, it would, she thought, and decided dazedly that when Michael had said his stepbrother was as rich as Croesus he hadn't been far wrong.

Guiltily reminded of Michael, she reached into her bag for her phone.

As though he'd forgotten their earlier conversation, Joel raised an eyebrow at her.

A shade awkwardly, she said, 'I really must talk to Michael before he sets off.'

His silvery-green eyes cool as a glacier, Joel asked, 'What explanation do you intend to give him for not being there?'

'I don't really know,' she admitted. She couldn't bring herself to tell him about Joel. 'But I can't just let him call and find me out.'

She dialled Michael's mobile and, when he answered promptly, blurted out, 'I'm sorry, but I won't be able to have lunch with you.'

'Why won't you?' he sounded cross.

'Something's cropped up and I'm going to be away for the weekend.'

'What's cropped up? Where are you going? Damn it, Bethany, the least you can do is explain.'

'Well, I—'

Taking the phone from her hand, Joel turned it off and dropped it into his own pocket.

Giving her a glinting smile, he said, 'You've told him you're not going to be there. Why make it complicated by trying to explain things?'

A little miffed by his high-handedness, she said, 'Don't you think he's entitled to an explanation?'

'You mean a truthful one?'

She felt her cheeks grow warm. The last thing she had wanted to do was tell Michael the truth.

'Perhaps he's *entitled* to one,' Joel went on caustically. 'But wouldn't it be *unsettling* for him, to say the least, to be told that the woman he's hoping to marry is going off to New York for the weekend with his stepbrother?'

Bethany bit her lip. She had always avoided dealing in lies and deception, but now she seemed to be caught up in that kind of situation. A situation she was totally unprepared for.

The events of the last few days had been so strange and unsettling, so wonderful in some ways, so traumatic in others...

'By the way,' Joel pursued as they reached the airport environs, 'when exactly did Michael ask you to marry him?'

'Last night when he took me home.'

'Not before you went up to Cumbria?'

'Certainly not... Surely you don't think—' She broke off.

'Don't think what?'

When, biting her lip, she stayed silent, he urged, 'Do go on.'

Taking a deep breath, she said, 'Think that if Michael had

already proposed and I'd had the slightest intention of marrying him, I would have...'

'Slept with me?' he finished for her. 'As you didn't know then that Michael and I were related, what was there to have stopped you?'

The impact of his words sent her reeling. He really *did* believe she was promiscuous. Something inside her, a hope for the future, a surviving dream perhaps, shrivelled up.

As they came to a halt at the terminal, he said with satisfaction, 'We've had a pretty good run through. We ought to be able to complete the formalities and take our slot with no hassle. Then, thanks to the time difference, we should be in Manhattan by early afternoon.'

'I've decided I've made a mistake. I don't want to go with you,' she informed him jerkily.

With no change of expression, he said, 'I'm afraid it's much too late for second thoughts.'

Setting her teeth, she repeated, 'I've no intention of going with you.'

He smiled, but it was sharp and it was fierce. 'So what do you intend to do?'

'I'll get a taxi back to London.'

'What's made you change your mind?'

'I hate to be thought promiscuous,' she blurted out. As he opened his mouth to speak, her grey eyes flashing, she cried, 'Don't bother to deny it. That's why you walked away that morning without a word.'

'I did no such thing,' he denied flatly. He added, 'And *I* hate to be thought a swine.'

Brought up short, she gaped at him foolishly. 'What do you mean?'

'After the night we'd just spent together, only a complete and utter swine would have walked away without a word.'

As hope was reborn like a phoenix from the ashes, she began urgently, 'Then why—'

'Something unexpected happened. Look, I'll explain later. There's no time now, here's the welcoming committee arriving.'

The 'welcoming committee' consisted of a smart young man, who greeted them deferentially, and one of his minions who took Bethany's case and Joel's leather briefcase.

Joel's arm at her waist, her thoughts in a turmoil, she allowed herself to be escorted into the airport buildings without further protest.

But as she went through the checks and procedures, she realized that even if there *was* an explanation, it didn't necessarily follow that it would make any difference to what he believed. It certainly wouldn't alter what he'd said in the car a short time ago…

After all the formalities had been completed, they were welcomed aboard the gleaming executive jet by a middle-aged quietly spoken steward with a French accent whom Joel addressed as Henri.

While Bethany's belongings were stowed away and the door closed and secured, they took their seats and fastened their belts before the plane began to taxi down the runway.

Take-off was smooth and effortless and, after climbing steeply, they were soon above the cloud layer and into bright sunshine.

When they levelled out, Joel unfastened his seat belt and said politely, 'I'd like to have a word with the pilot, if you'll excuse me?'

'Of course.'

'Perhaps you'd care to take a look round? Oh, and in the meantime if there's anything you want, just ask Henri.'

As Joel went into the cockpit, the white-jacketed steward came from the galley and showed Bethany into an attractive lounge area.

She refused the champagne and caviare he offered but accepted a cup of coffee, which appeared as if by magic and proved to be excellent.

While she sipped, she looked around her. She had never travelled in a privately owned jet before and was bowled over by the opulence of her surroundings.

A cream cushioned couch and two armchairs, an inlaid coffee table between them, stood on a sumptuous carpet, while to the right was a video screen and music centre. Opposite, hung a beautiful Monet whose colours echoed the delicate blues and pinks and lilacs of the carpet.

The only utilitarian thing there was a small businesslike desk with a laptop computer and a black leather swivel chair.

Her coffee finished, she put her cup and saucer on the table and went to explore further.

At the far end of the cabin, next to a well-appointed shower room and toilet, was a small, but luxurious bedroom.

Looking at the bed, she frowned. Why did a businessman need a bed with black silk sheets that fairly breathed seduction, unless he regularly mixed business with pleasure?

Perhaps he did. Maybe she was just one of many who'd been only too willing to accompany him on his 'business' trips.

Though she knew from his sexual expertise that he was an experienced man with a powerful libido, he had a certain asceticism, and she knew—or *thought* she knew—that he was capable of exercising a remarkable degree of restraint and self-control.

Did that self-control, that apparent restraint, that touch of asceticism, serve to conceal the soul of a libertine?

It was a far from pleasant thought and she faced the undeniable fact that she'd been a fool to come. But she didn't *have* to sleep with him. She could always refuse.

Shaken to realize just what kind of man she might have fallen in love with, she made her way back to the lounge and sat down in one of the armchairs.

She had only been there a short time when the door opened and Joel appeared. He put his briefcase on the desk and, taking off his jacket, dropped it over the back of the swivel chair, saying cheerfully, 'Jack says it should be a good, smooth flight.'

Then, his eyes fixed on her face, he queried, 'What's wrong?'

'Nothing's wrong,' she denied swiftly.

'Something's upset you,' he said with certainty. 'What is it?'

'I was just wondering why you needed a bed,' she said in a rush.

He raised a well-marked brow. 'You mean apart from to sleep in?'

'Is that all you use it for?'

His eyes gleamed silver. 'It's all I've used it for up to press, though I must confess I was hoping this trip might be different.'

'I imagine every trip is *different*.' There was scorn in her voice.

He raised a brow. 'You think I regularly mix business and pleasure?'

'Don't you?'

'As a rule I keep business and pleasure strictly separate. *You* are the exception to that rule and, incidentally, the only woman I've ever brought aboard.'

His words held the ring of truth. And, thinking so little of her, why would he bother to lie?

'But would any man on his own choose to have black silk sheets?' She spoke the thought aloud.

'I've never asked for black silk sheets. I leave the details to Henri.'

Drily, he added, 'Perhaps he's trying to live up to the millionaire image? Or maybe his taste runs to the exotic? Either way, if black silk sheets bother you, I'll ask to have them replaced by white linen.'

'They don't bother me,' she said hurriedly. 'As I've absolutely no intention of—'

A knock at the door made her stop in mid-sentence and a moment later the soft-footed steward wheeled in a lunch trolley.

'Thank you, Henri,' Joel said briskly. 'We can serve ourselves.'

Turning to Bethany he asked, 'What would you like? Seafood? Chicken? Salad?'

'I'm not hungry.' It was the truth. She felt too churned up to eat.

'Did you have any breakfast?'

'No,' she admitted.

'Then, as I object to eating alone, I'd like you to join me.'

'I'm really not hungry,' she said tersely.

'You're plenty slim enough, and going without food this long can't be good for you.'

When she stayed stubbornly silent, he sighed. 'Well, I can't force you to eat…'

She was just feeling a sense of triumph when he went on blandly, 'But after looking forward to having someone to share things with, I'll have to think of some other activity we can indulge in.'

As, her heart picking up speed, she stared at him, he added, 'I'm reluctant to ask Henri to change the sheets before lunch, so it's just as well they won't bother you.'

Agitation brought her to her feet. 'You can't force me to go to bed with you either.'

'I wouldn't bet on that if I were you. Though *force* is hardly the right word…'

Rising in one lithe movement, he eased her backwards, leaning into her so that she was trapped between his body and the bulkhead. Then, one arm each side of her, he bent until his lips were almost brushing hers and added softly, 'Persuade is nearer the mark.'

She could smell the clean scent of his skin mingling with his spicy aftershave and, shivers running down her spine, she threatened, 'If you don't let me go I'll call for Henri.'

He laughed as if genuinely amused. 'Do you imagine that a man who is dissolute enough to have black silk sheets on his bed won't employ a steward who is conveniently deaf?'

'You said the sheets weren't your choice,' she said in a strangled voice.

'Did you believe me?'

Angry that he was laughing at her, she snapped, 'No, I didn't,' and tried to break free, but his arms were like steel bars.

He touched his lips to the side of her neck. 'Well, it happens to be the truth. Though, having agreed to spend the weekend with me, I would have thought you'd take silk sheets in your stride.'

'You make it sound as if I'm in the habit of spending weekends with men...'

He leant back and raised a quizzical brow. 'And you're not?'

'No, I'm not.'

'You mean I'm an exception?' He laughed.

'Yes.'

'So tell me why, having agreed to come with me, you now don't want to sleep with me.'

'Because you think I'm promiscuous,' she burst out.

He smiled languidly. 'But I've already said I don't think that.'

She shook her head. 'That isn't what you said. You simply denied that you'd walked out on me.'

'Which again is the truth, but I suppose you don't believe that either.'

Wanting to believe him, she said distractedly, 'You said you'd explain... I don't know what to believe until I've heard that explanation.'

'Then let's call a truce and over lunch I'll tell you exactly what happened.'

'Even if I believe you it won't make any difference. It won't alter the way you feel about me. It won't alter what you said in the car.'

Innocently, he asked, 'What did I say in the car?'

The cynical words seemed burnt into her brain. 'You said, "As you didn't know then that Michael and I were related, what was there to have stopped you?"'

He smiled to himself, amused that she could recollect what he had said, word for word. 'That was a question, not an accusation. Perhaps I expected you to answer something like, Because I'm not that kind of woman... I have a conscience... A code of morals...'

'If I had said any of those things, would you have believed me?'

'I might have, except for one thing...'

She knew quite well what that one thing was. She had agreed to spend the weekend with him, though she still hadn't given Michael a final answer.

Clearly, she said, 'If I'd had any intention of marrying Michael I would never have agreed to come away with you, whether you were related or not.'

He cocked his head to one side. 'So you haven't any intention of marrying him?'

'No, I haven't. I tried to tell him so at the time but he wouldn't take no for an answer.'

'If you hadn't any intention of marrying him, why didn't you admit it when I asked?'

'Because you didn't ask. You *told* me to say no. I thought you were too arrogant by half. You put my back up,' she said emphatically.

'I see.' Then, quick as a rattlesnake striking, 'Why did you turn Michael down?'

'Because I don't love him.'

'What's love got to do with it?'

She looked down shyly. 'As far as I'm concerned, everything. I would never marry a man I didn't love.'

Studying her through long thick lashes tipped with gold—lashes any woman might have envied—he began thoughtfully, 'Tell me something…'

Thrown by the way he was looking at her, she said uncertainly, 'What?'

'Why did you agree to come on this weekend jaunt?'

After a momentary hesitation, she answered as casually as possible, 'Because I wanted to be with you.' It was the truth, yet not the whole truth.

He straightened and, taking her hand, raised it to his lips and kissed the palm. 'That's a good enough answer. Suppose we take it from there and see where we get to?'

She half nodded.

Touching his lips to hers, he asked lightly, 'Now what would you like to eat? And don't tell me you're not hungry.'

'I wouldn't dare.'

He laughed. 'So what's it to be?'

'A little seafood and salad, please.'

When they both had a plate of fresh salmon, prawns and lobster and a glass of chilled white wine, she reminded him, 'You said you would explain.'

He raised his wineglass and took a sip before beginning. 'I woke quite early and it was barely light when I left to fetch my car. You were fast asleep and—'

She looked up at him with innocent grey eyes. 'Why didn't you wake me?'

'I had every intention of coming straight back, but when I got outside I found there was an emergency. The local mountain rescue team had been called out to an injured climber who'd fallen into a ravine the previous night when he was caught in the mist.

'In the early hours of the morning, when the mist started to lift, his companion managed to make it as far as Dundale and raise the alarm.

'The rescue team were desperately short-handed. Two of their men were down with flu and the caretaker, who sometimes goes out with them, was hardly able to move for rheumatism.

'As I know those fells like the back of my hand, and I've been out with the team before, I agreed to go with them.' He leant forward and brushed her cheek affectionately with the back of his hand.

'I would have stopped to explain, but there wasn't a second to lose. In those conditions any delay could have made the difference between life and death. I asked the caretaker to tell you what had happened, and say that if you could wait at the Dundale Inn I'd try to be there by lunch time.

'Presumably he didn't tell you?'

'No... I didn't see him.' If only she had spoken to the man before she'd left, it would have saved her so much pain.

'In the event,' Joel went on, 'the climber was badly injured and it took so long to bring him safely down that it was almost three o'clock when I finally got to Dundale.

'I asked for a Miss Seaton.' His smile crooked, he added, 'Needless to say, there was no Miss Seaton in the register, only a Mr and Mrs Feldon.'

So that was how he'd known.

'I presumed that was why you hadn't waited,' he added evenly.

As she half shook her head, he said, 'Tell me, if the caretaker *had* given you my message, would you have waited?'

'Yes,' she answered without hesitation. She would have waited even if it had meant catching a train back to London.

After a moment, he pursued, 'So are you satisfied that I wasn't rotten enough to just walk out on you?'

'Yes,' she said in a small voice. 'I'm sorry.'

They finished their lunch without speaking, each, it seemed, busy with their thoughts.

Henri had removed the trolley and served coffee before Joel broke the silence to ask reflectively, 'How long have you known Michael?'

'About three months.'

'How many times have you been to Lanervic Square?'

'That was the only time.'

'He hasn't taken you there before?'

'No.' Something about Joel's expression made her ask, 'Why should he?'

Then, putting her cup down with a rattle, 'You think we've been going there to spend the night?'

'It did cross my mind that as each of you are encumbered with a flatmate it would have been... shall we say... convenient.'

Tightly, she said, 'I've already told you that I've never slept with Michael.'

'Then if you weren't intending to spend the night with him, why did you go?'

'He wanted me to—' Seeing the wolfish look that had appeared on Joel's face, she broke off, her thoughts suddenly racing, a serious doubt in her mind.

For some reason, encountering his stepbrother at Lanervic Square had upset Michael almost as much as it had upset her. All the colour had drained from his face when Joel had asked him what he was doing there.

But surely if the house was his, he had every right to be there and take who he pleased? Unless it wasn't officially his and he shouldn't have been disposing of the contents until probate had been granted?

'You were saying?' Joel prompted smoothly.

Unwilling to mention the real reason for her visit and perhaps get Michael into trouble, she stuck with the story he'd told. 'He wanted me to see where he used to live.'

For an instant a hard, angry look darkened Joel's handsome face. Then a shutter came down and he said coolly, 'Yes, if I remember rightly, that's what he said at the time.'

Jumping in with both feet, she added, 'I understand the house is his now?'

'So it is…' Joel agreed.

She breathed a sigh of relief. So Michael *had* been speaking the truth. For a minute she had begun to doubt him, to wonder if he could have been lying.

'And he's very anxious to sell it,' Joel went on. 'But, because of the terms of the will, he can't do anything with it for the next two years… Apart from live in it, that is. And he doesn't want to do that.'

He paused, his eyes on her face, as though expecting some comment.

Carefully, she said, 'Yes, he told me that too.' She added, 'Two years seems a long time to wait.'

'Michael's always had a fondness for the good life—wine, women and a predilection for gambling—which makes him an easy prey for the more unscrupulous…'

Bethany heard the ring of steel in his voice as he went on, 'Our grandmother knew that he needed to be protected, so she gave me control until he's twenty-five, in the hope that he would get a bit of sense before then and not throw it all away.'

CHAPTER FIVE

AFTER a few seconds, when Bethany made no comment, Joel changed tack. 'So where did you and Michael meet?'

'He came into the shop early one evening,' she admitted unguardedly.

The sudden tightening of Joel's mouth convinced her she was on dangerous ground and she found herself wondering, as Michael wasn't supposed to sell the house until he was twenty-five—even after probate had been granted—did that go for the contents as well?

Maybe *that* was why, when she'd asked, 'How many pieces do you want to part with?' he'd said, 'One... Two at the most. Otherwise it might be—' Had he been going to say *obvious* and thought better of it?

'What did he come into the shop for?' Joel asked, his voice casual.

Worried now, she lied awkwardly, 'I imagine it was just to browse.'

'I wasn't aware that he was interested in antiques,' Joel observed mildly.

'I don't think he is,' she admitted.

'Then why go into an antiques shop to browse?'

'Sometimes people who know nothing about antiques will

come in to choose a piece of silver or porcelain as, say, a wedding gift,' she told him truthfully.

'I see. So what happened when he came in?'

'We… we got talking.' She began to feel a little frustrated.

'What did you talk about?'

Feeling as though she was being given the third degree, she prevaricated, 'I really don't remember.'

'Perhaps that was when he told you he'd inherited his grand-mother's house?'

'It might have been,' she admitted.

'But he didn't mention me?'

She shook her head. 'No. I didn't even know he had a step-brother until the other night.'

On a sudden impulse, she added, 'I gather you and he don't get on too well?'

'No, unfortunately not…'

She saw by the bleakness of Joel's expression that he cared about his young stepbrother and the poor relations between them.

'I've done my best to look after his interests but, as you can imagine, he bitterly resents the fact that I have control… Which makes things difficult, without an added complication.'

Painfully aware that *she* was the 'added complication' Bethany said carefully, 'Rather than make things any more dif-ficult, I could step out of both your lives, make certain I never saw either of you again…'

At that instant there was a knock at the door.

Frowning a little, Joel called, 'Come in.'

When the steward appeared, he said shortly, 'Yes, Henri, what is it?'

'Captain Ross sends his apologies, sir, but could he take another look at the chart you showed him earlier? Apparently he has a query.'

'I'll only be a minute,' Joel said to Bethany and, while the steward began to gather up the coffee cups, took a small flip chart from his briefcase and vanished into the forward cabin.

Henri had started to follow Joel, the loaded tray in his hands, when he caught the protruding corner of the briefcase and toppled it on to the floor, spilling its contents.

Murmuring an apology, he was about to put the tray back on the table when Bethany said, 'It's all right, Henri, I'll pick it up.'

'Thank you, miss.' A moment later the door slid to behind him.

Crouching, she righted the briefcase and began to gather together the various papers. As she did so, her fingers touched something metallic.

Her heart suddenly pounding, and feeling as though she had just been kicked in the solar plexus, Bethany found herself looking down at an intricate gold bracelet set with deep red stones.

Rooted to the spot, she was still staring at it when the door opened and Joel reappeared.

Following the direction of her gaze, he observed, 'Ah, you've found it.' He strode over and, taking her arm, helped her to her feet.

Feeling guilty for no reason, she explained uncomfortably, 'Your case got knocked off the desk and I was just...'

'Yes, Henri mentioned it,' he said evenly.

Picking up the bracelet, he took her hand and slipped it on to her wrist.

While he replaced the contents of the briefcase and fastened it, she stared at the bracelet. 'I thought I'd left it at The Dunbeck. I tried ringing the caretaker, but I couldn't get any answer.'

Then, lifting puzzled grey eyes to his face, 'I don't understand how it came to be in your briefcase.'

'I brought it along with the intention of returning it to you.'

'But where did you get it?' she questioned.

'You'd left it in the bathroom, so on an impulse I picked it up.' He shrugged.

'Why did you keep it?'

Just for a split second he looked disconcerted, before he said lightly, 'You could call it safeguarding my interests. If you didn't happen to wait for me at the Dundale Inn, at least I'd have an excuse to see you again.'

She felt a rush of gladness. He had wanted, *intended,* to see her again. Yet, even as warmth spread through her, part of her brain insisted that his explanation wasn't logical. Somewhere there was a flaw in it.

Before she could pin it down, he said, 'But, to get back to what we were saying before Henri came in. You had just offered to step out of both Michael's life and mine... Make certain you never saw either of us again. Would you be prepared to do that?'

She hesitated. The thought of never seeing Joel again made her feel as though she was mortally wounded. But if that was what he wanted now he'd had time to think about it and consider the possible repercussions...

Lifting her chin, she said quietly, 'Yes. If that's what you want.'

He pierced her with his gaze. 'It isn't.'

As she looked at him, hoping against hope that she'd heard right, he went on, 'I happen to want you in my bed, in my life. In fact I wouldn't be prepared to let you go, even for Michael's sake.'

Her heart swelled.

As though pushing away any lingering concern, Joel took her hand and, a glint in his eye, suggested softly, 'Speaking of bed, what if I ask Henri to change the sheets?'

Embarrassed, she begged. 'Oh, no... Please don't.'

'Does that mean you still don't want to go to bed with me?'

She shook her head. 'No, it means I've decided I like black silk sheets.'

Laughing, he said, 'I do love a woman who isn't afraid to change her mind. I'll just tell Henri that we're going to bed for a couple of hours and don't want to be disturbed.'

'Oh, but what will he think?' She turned away shyly.

'He won't think anything. And, if he does, he's French and a man of the world.'

Seeing she still looked uncomfortable, Joel said a shade mockingly, 'Don't worry, I'll make sure he doesn't class you as a lady of easy virtue.'

Refusing to rise to the bait, she stayed silent and watched as he slid aside the door and disappeared into the forward section.

He came back a minute or so later carrying a bottle of vintage champagne and a couple of glasses. With a lazy smile he said, 'Henri seemed to think champagne was fitting, and I didn't want to disappoint him.'

Having unwired the cork and eased it out with a satisfying pop, Joel filled the flutes with a foaming gush of wine. When the bubbles had subsided he handed her a glass and raised his own. 'To us.'

Then, finding it a sweet amusement to tease her, 'Here's to joining the Mile-High Club.'

'The Mile-High Club?' She looked puzzled.

'A mere handful of people who are able to make love more than a mile above the earth's surface.'

Feeling her colour rise, she said, 'Oh… I see…'

An innate shyness making her unable to meet his laughing eyes, she looked down at her glass and watched the bubbles rising in a golden shower to the surface before taking her first sip.

The wine was cool and crisp on her tongue, making her whole body tingle as it went down. Or was that simply excitement and anticipation?

As soon as their glasses were empty, he put them both on the table and, taking her hand, led her through to the bedroom.

He lowered the blinds, shutting out the brightness, before taking the pins from her hair and letting the dark, silky mass tumble round her shoulders. Then, burying his face in it, he breathed in its perfume while his hands traced her slender curves.

When he began to undress her it was slow and erotic, as he caressed and tasted each new piece of creamy flesh until she was totally naked and on fire for him.

Murmuring how lovely she was, how much he wanted her, he held her hips between his hands and leaned her gently back until she was on the bed. Then, his eyes heavy-lidded and sensual, he stroked his fingertips up and down the smooth satiny skin of her inner thighs.

Her breathing quickened as he explored further, his probing touch light, delicate, yet already producing the most exquisite sensations.

When he brought her right to the very brink and then drew back, it was all she could do to prevent herself from begging.

Her stomach was still tied in knots when he put his hands beneath her buttocks and, lifting her higher, bent his head. The flick of his tongue sent her up like a young supernova exploding into being.

As she plucked a star from the firmament of pleasure, he gently eased her head on to the pillow and settled her into a more comfortable position, before stepping away.

When she floated back to earth and opened her eyes, he was stripping off his own clothes. The black silk sheets felt cool and exotic against her heated flesh as she lay watching him.

With broad shoulders and lean hips and carrying not an ounce of spare weight, he had a superb male physique. Muscles rippled beneath a clear, lightly bronzed skin that gleamed like oiled silk, making her want to stroke it. His legs were straight, with a scattering of golden hair, the line of his spine long and elegant.

When he took off his dark silk boxer shorts, though she had thought herself more than satisfied, her stomach clenched in anticipation.

Glancing up and seeing her watching him, he smiled at her, a smile that was neither self-conscious nor vain. He looked assured, confident, like a man completely at ease with his own masculinity.

He was a passionate lover, yet he made love with a care and sensitivity that showed he put his partner's pleasure ahead of his own.

After—sated and content—she had slept for a while in his arms, he wakened her with a kiss and made love to her again, this time displaying an inventive ardour that had them rolling in an erotic tangle of limbs on the black silk sheets.

When she awoke for the second time, she was alone in the bed. A glance at her watch told her they must be approaching their destination.

Her clothes had been placed on a gold velvet boudoir chair and, gathering them up, she went through to the adjoining shower room.

It appeared that Joel had already showered. The clean, fresh scent of his shower gel still hung in the air and fine drops of water spangled the glass.

Swiftly she took her hair up into a knot and stepped under the flow of hot water.

When she was dried and dressed, her dark hair once more in a smooth coil, she glanced at her reflection in the mirror. A tinge of apricot colour lay along her high cheekbones and the smoke-grey eyes that looked back at her had a lit-from-within radiance.

Satisfied that she no longer looked like a ghost, and needed no help from cosmetics, she made her way back to the lounge.

There was no sign of Joel and she was wondering whether to go in search of him when there was a tap at the door and Henri came in carrying a tray set with delicate china.

She felt her face grow warm.

But, his eyes respectfully lowered, he informed her, 'Mr McAlister asked me to say that we will be landing in just over half an hour. He's with Captain Ross at the moment, but he'll be joining you shortly. In the meantime he thought you might like a cup of tea.'

'Thank you, I would.'

Putting the tray down, the steward enquired, 'Would madam prefer milk or lemon?'

'Milk, please.'

When he'd poured the pale amber liquid, he enquired solicitously, 'Would madam care for anything to eat?'

'Oh, no, thank you. The tea will do fine.'

He gave a half bow and, eyes still lowered, made his way out.

Feeling a little dazed, Bethany stared after him. Where earlier the steward had been merely polite, this time his manner had been positively deferential and she noted with surprise that he had changed her mode of address from miss to madam.

What on earth had Joel said to him? she wondered as she sat and sipped her tea. She was still wondering a few minutes later when the door opened and Joel came in.

Tilting her face proprietorially, he kissed her and said, 'You look quite glowing. Making love in the afternoon must suit you.'

Watching her colour rise, he added, 'In this day and age it's rare to see a woman blush so delightfully.'

Knowing that if she allowed it he could have her in a perpetual state of turmoil, she tried to ignore his teasing and, in an attempt to hide how much he could affect her, said as coolly as possible, 'I understand we'll be landing soon.'

He glanced at his watch. 'That's right. By the way, I take it you couldn't fault Henri's demeanour?'

She shook her head. 'In fact, he was so deferential I couldn't help but wonder what you'd said to him.'

'I made it clear that you were special, not just some casual girlfriend.' He smirked.

If only he meant it. Her voice a little uneven, she asked, 'Why did you tell him that?'

'You were afraid of being classed as 'easy' so it seemed to be the best way to ensure his respect…

'Incidentally, I spoke to my housekeeper a short time ago and, as we'll be sharing a room, I told her the same.' His tone was casual, but the hint of authority made her stomach flip.

Briskly, he added, 'Now, as we're due to land in a matter of minutes, I suggest we get belted up.'

The landing was a smooth one and in no time at all they had cleared the runway and were taxiing towards the airport buildings.

When all the formalities were over, with a great deal of pomp and circumstance, they were escorted out to a waiting limousine.

It was a bitterly cold afternoon but still bright and sunny, with a sky the pale, delicate blue of forget-me-nots, criss-crossed with the gauzy white ribbons of vapour trails.

Standing to attention by the sleek silver car, the chauffeur gave them a smart salute. 'Good afternoon, sir, madam, nice to have you back. I hope you had a good flight?'

'Very good, thank you, Tom. How's the traffic?'

'Much as usual, Mr McAlister. Could be worse. Shouldn't be too late getting home.'

'That's good.'

When Joel had fastened their seat belts and they were heading for Manhattan, Bethany remarked, 'You haven't told me where you live.'

'I live in an old brownstone on Mulberry Street, Lower Manhattan, a house I originally bought and had refurbished for my mother.'

'Oh…' She was surprised.

Picking up that surprise, he asked quizzically, 'What did you expect? Some glass and chromium penthouse overlooking Central Park?'

That was almost exactly what she had expected.

When she admitted it, he grinned and said, 'Don't look so sheepish. A lot of people who don't know me well make that mistake.

'And, as a matter of fact, I did have a Fifth Avenue penthouse for a while; it was only after my mother died that I moved into Mulberry Street.'

'And you like living there?'

'It suits me very well. When I first bought the brownstone it was in a poor state, but after it was refurbished it became a pleasant place to live…'

Then, on her wavelength as he often was, he observed drily, 'I see you're wondering why I didn't simply buy a house that didn't need refurbishing. And of course I could have done. But my mother wanted one that could be restored to its original character, so this place was ideal.

'There was a great deal of skilled work to do when I first bought it, and it took a dedicated team six months to turn it back into the beautiful house it had once been.'

Bethany smiled at him adoringly. 'So your mother was pleased with it?'

'Oh, yes, she loved it. Just before she died she told me that the two years she had lived there had been the happiest of her life...'

In spite of the heavy traffic it didn't seem long before Manhattan's skyscrapers came into view and, as always, Bethany was enthralled.

Watching her face, he asked, 'Glad to be back?'

Suddenly full up, she nodded. No matter what the future held, she was in New York with the man she loved. It was a wonderful thought.

By the time they reached Mulberry Street, a pleasant tree-lined street not far from Greenwich Village, the sun had gone down and lights were starting to twinkle in the blue dusk.

When they drew to a halt by the kerb, Joel helped Bethany out and, while the chauffeur dealt with the luggage, escorted her up the front stairs and into the lighted hallway.

The walls had been painted ivory, while the floor and stairs were carpeted in rich burgundy. The line of the staircase was elegant, the cherry wood banisters and newel posts polished to gleaming perfection.

As she glanced around her, a door opened and a neatly dressed middle-aged woman appeared.

Smiling at them both, she said, 'Welcome home. It's nice to see you back, Mr McAlister. I hope you had an enjoyable flight?'

'Most enjoyable,' Joel assured her, giving Bethany a wicked sideways glance that made her cheeks grow warm.

Then, taking her hand, he said, 'Bethany, darling, this is Mrs Brannigan, Tom's wife and a housekeeper *par excellence*.'

Clearly pleased by the compliment, Mrs Brannigan gave them both a beaming smile and said, 'It's nice to meet you, Miss Seaton.'

Though shaken by the *darling*, Bethany managed to smile back.

'Will you be wanting dinner?' the housekeeper pursued.

As Bethany hesitated, Joel answered, 'No thanks, Molly. I thought we'd eat out.'

'Then a cup of tea, perhaps?'

'That would fit the bill nicely.'

When the housekeeper had taken their coats and hung them in the hall cupboard, a hand at Bethany's waist, Joel suggested, 'While we're waiting, let me give you a quick tour of the place, so you feel at home…

'Molly and Tom have the ground floor,' he went on as they crossed the hall, 'and the kitchens are at the rear. This is the living room and, next to it, my office…'

The living room, a spacious, attractive room, was classically decorated in warm shades of red and cream, while his study was a restful mint-green.

As he showed her round, it was apparent that Joel's interior designer was an artist who liked clear, clean colours.

There were pocket doors with exquisitely etched birds and flowers, dark, gleaming woodwork and rich, jewel-bright colours: sapphire and jade, gold and garnet, purple and lapis lazuli.

It was as beautiful and vivid as a stained glass window and, though she had always tended to be conservative when it came to colour, Bethany was caught up by a wave of pleasure.

'What do you think?' he asked as they returned to the living room.

Turning shining eyes on him, she answered, 'It's absolutely wonderful.'

He smiled. 'I'm glad you like it.'

So far most of the furniture had been made up of carefully chosen antiques, but the suite was up-to-date and comfortable-looking, and the music centre and television were state-of-the-art.

As they sat down on the cushioned couch there was a tap at the door and the housekeeper came in with their tea.

'Could I have a word, Mr McAlister?'

'Of course, Molly. What is it?'

After a momentary hesitation, the housekeeper said, 'Miss Lampton rang again this morning to ask when you would be back.'

'Did you tell her?'

'Yes… I tried to put her off, but she was very insistent.' Molly's lips tightened with disapproval. 'I hope I did the right thing.'

He sat back. 'That's fine. Don't worry about it.'

Looking relieved, the housekeeper went, closing the door behind her.

Joel poured the tea and handed Bethany a cup before asking, 'How are you coping with the jet lag?'

'Fine. As a rule when I come to the States I try to stay awake until bedtime, and I find that usually works well.' She sipped her tea.

'Good. Fancy going to the Trocadero tonight?'

Bethany was well aware that the Fifth Avenue nightclub was *the* place to be seen, and she'd heard it said that if you weren't royalty, a top celebrity, or a multi-millionaire it was next to impossible to get a table.

She was shaken to realize afresh that the man she loved belonged in that bracket. It put him among the elite, and right out of her league.

Suddenly she wished passionately that he wasn't wealthy, but just an ordinary man. If he didn't have money, there might be some chance of *staying* in his life—working alongside him, buying a small house, having his children, building a future together…

'You're looking very serious.' Joel's voice broke into her thoughts. 'If the Trocadero isn't a good choice, we can—'

'Oh, it *is*,' she broke in. 'Except that I've nothing to wear.'

'What about the little black cocktail dress I saw you packing? That will—'

He broke off as the door opened and a tall, slender girl in her late teens or early twenties, wearing a mink coat and a soft matching hat, came in.

As he rose to his feet, she cried, 'Joel, darling! So you're back at last. You'll never know how I've missed you!'

Her accent was upper-class and an aura of wealth and breeding and privilege hung round her like a jewelled cloak.

Polished and sophisticated, trailing a cloud of French perfume, she crossed the room and, throwing her arms around his neck, stood on tiptoe to kiss him on the lips.

Sitting frozen, watching how she pressed herself against him, Bethany had no doubt at all that they were lovers.

After a moment or two, he reached up to unwind her arms.

'How are you, Tara?' he asked coolly. 'You're looking very well.'

That was an understatement, Bethany thought. A natural redhead, with an oval face, huge blue eyes fringed with long, dark lashes and a full passionate mouth painted a rich coral, the newcomer looked like a vivid oil painting.

Beside her, Bethany felt drab and colourless.

For the first time in her life, she found herself envying another woman. Not only because of her glowing looks, but because of her class and her secure place in Joel's world.

This was the sort of woman he would doubtless choose to marry.

Sounding a shade uncertain, Tara asked, 'Is Michael with you?'

Almost curtly, Joel answered, 'No.'

Looking relieved, she rushed on, 'Why on earth didn't you let me know you were coming? I'd have met you at the airport.

'Oh darling, it seems an age since I saw you. I'd started to think you were never coming back—'

Joel's quiet voice cut through the flow. 'I didn't hear the doorbell.'

She held up a fob with a key attached. 'I still have my key.'

He took it neatly from her fingers and dropped it into his pocket.

Pouting prettily, she coaxed, 'You're not still cross with me, are you?'

His voice was cool as her replied. 'Not at all.'

'Then why are you being so horrid? I told you at the time it didn't mean a thing. It was just a bit of fun. We happened to be at the same party and we got high. He asked me back here, and I—'

'Perhaps you should save the explanations for when we're alone?'

Bethany had got to her feet and was heading blindly for the door, when Joel stopped her in her tracks. 'Please don't go.' His voice cracked like a whip.

Tara looked at Bethany as if noticing her for the first time. Then, clearly dismissing her as being of little consequence, she turned back to Joel and, caressing his chin with one coral-tipped finger, coaxed, 'Why don't you take me to the Trocadero tonight and I'll—'

'I already have arrangements for tonight,' he broke in smoothly.

She pouted. 'Can't you alter them?'

'No.'

'Tomorrow, then... It's Lisa's party, and she told me you'd promised both her and her father you'd go. Brian was going to escort me, but I can easily put him off. If you pick me up at seven—'

'I'm afraid I can't do that.'

Obviously getting angry and frustrated, she demanded, 'Why not?'

'Because I'll be escorting my guest...'

As Tara's eyes swivelled in Bethany's direction, he added, 'Now, as you two ladies haven't met, allow me to introduce you...'

While Bethany stood numbly, he crossed the room to take her

hand and draw her forward. 'Darling, this is Tara Lampton...
Tara, Bethany Seaton.'

Guessing that the endearment was intended to make the other
woman jealous, or to bring her to heel, Bethany said through stiff
lips, 'How do you do?'

Tara gave her a look that, if looks could kill, would have
shrivelled her up and, without a word, turned on her heel and
stormed out.

A moment later the front door slammed.

His face expressionless, Joel drew Bethany back to the couch
and, sitting down by her side, observed, 'I'm sorry Tara was so
rude to you. She's always been something of a spoilt brat.'

Without meaning to, Bethany found herself saying accus-
ingly, 'You were trying to make her jealous.'

He lifted a level brow. 'Oh? What makes you think that?'

'You called me darling.'

'I called you darling earlier, if you remember, and I can assure
you that I wasn't trying to make my housekeeper jealous.'

Knowing he was laughing at her, Bethany bit her lip and said
nothing further.

'Now, where were we? Oh, yes, the Trocadero. If you're not
happy wearing the dress you brought I can phone Joshua
Dellon and get a selection of dresses sent round. I have an
account there and—'

'Oh, no!'

'There's no need to look quite so horrified. I've bought clothes
for women before now.'

I just bet you have, she thought. Aloud, she said stiffly, 'Thank
you, but I prefer to buy my own clothes and, as there's no way
I could afford any Joshua Dellon designs, I'll stick with what I've
got. That is if you still want to take me?'

He looked puzzled. 'Why shouldn't I still want to take you?'

'Your girlfriend wasn't happy about it.' Bethany found she could barely meet his gaze.

'My ex-girlfriend,' he corrected. 'It was over several weeks ago, before I went back to London.'

Recalling how possessive the redhead had been, Bethany said drily, '*She* didn't seem to think so.'

'Even if she doesn't want a man any longer, Tara can't bear to lose him.'

'I got the impression that she did want you. That she's still in love with you.'

Using a single finger to tilt her chin, he asked quizzically, 'Jealous?'

'Certainly not,' she denied emphatically.

'So *you're* not in love with me?'

Ambushed by the unexpected question, she gazed at him in silence.

'Well?' he pressed.

Somehow she gathered herself and asked, 'If I said I was, would you believe me?'

'Would you expect me to?'

'No,' she admitted.

His teeth gleamed as he smiled. 'So you're *not* in love with me?'

She took a deep breath. 'No.'

'Well, at least you're more honest than Tara, who swore she loved me madly. Whereas I suspect that all she really wanted was my money and the kind of lifestyle I can offer.'

Remembering the mink, and the air of wealth and breeding the girl had exuded, Bethany said, 'She appeared to already have those things.'

'She's always been privileged. Her father's an English baronet and comparatively wealthy, but last year, after his first wife died, he remarried.

'Tara and her stepmother don't get along too well. And, even if they did, as they both let money run through their fingers like water, it's doubtful if Sir William could afford to keep them both.

'So you see there's pressure on Tara to find a rich and doting husband and move out.' His silvery-green eyes gleaming, he added, 'She seemed to think I'd fit the bill…'

CHAPTER SIX

'But *you* don't.' Bethany held her breath.

'No, I don't,' Joel said flatly.

'You don't intend to marry?'

'Oh, yes, I have every intention of getting married. And before too long. But not to Tara. She's a beautiful woman, and I've no doubt that she would make a glamorous and stimulating wife. But unfortunately not a faithful one.'

Married to a man like Joel, Bethany thought, who in their right mind would want to stray? Aloud she ventured, 'And being faithful is important to you?'

'Yes.' His answer was uncompromising. 'With all this sexual freedom it may seem an old-fashioned concept, but when I marry I want a wife I can trust and respect. Not one I have to continually watch and wonder who else she's going to bed with…'

But would that cut both ways? Bethany wondered.

Displaying that unnerving ability to walk in and out of her mind, he said, 'I only need one woman in my life and when I'm satisfied that I've found the right one I have every intention of being faithful to her.'

If only she was that lucky woman.

But circumstances had already destroyed any faint chance she *might* have stood had things happened differently. All she was

IMANI
ROMANCE

An Important Message from the Publisher

Dear Reader,

If you'd enjoy reading contemporary African-American love stories filled with drama and passion, then let us send you two free Kimani Romance™ novels. These books will keep it real with true-to-life African-American characters that turn up the heat and sizzle with passion.

By the way, you'll also get two surprise gifts with your two free books! Please enjoy the free books and gifts with our compliments...

Linda Gill

Publisher, Kimani Press

Peel off Seal and Place Inside...

We'd like to send you two free books to introduce you to our brand-new line – Kimani Romance™! These novels feature strong, sexy women, and African-American heroes that are charming, loving, and true. Our authors fill each page with exceptional dialogue, exciting plot twists, and enough sizzling romance to keep you riveted until the very end!

KIMANI ROMANCE ... LOVE'S ULTIMATE DESTINATION

Your two books have a combined cover price of $11.98 in the U.S. and $13.98 in Canada, but are yours **FREE!** We'll even send you two wonderful surprise gifts. You can't lose!

2 Free Bonus Gifts!

We'll send you two wonderful surprise gifts, absolutely FREE, just for giving KIMANI ROMANCE books a try! Don't miss out —— MAIL THE REPLY CARD TODAY!

www.KimaniPress.com

THE EDITOR'S "THANK YOU" FREE GIFTS INCLUDE:

▶ Two NEW Kimani Romance™ Novels
▶ Two exciting surprise gifts

YES! I have placed my Editor's "thank you" Free Gifts seal in the space provided at right. Please send me 2 FREE books, and my 2 FREE Mystery Gifts. I understand that I am under no obligation to purchase anything further, as explained on the back of this card.

PLACE FREE GIFTS SEAL HERE

▶ DETACH AND MAIL CARD TODAY! ▶

168 XDL EF2J   368 XDL EF2U

FIRST NAME	LAST NAME

ADDRESS

APT.#	CITY

STATE/PROV.	ZIP/POSTAL CODE

Thank You!

(KR-PAS-11/06)

The Reader Service — Here's How It Works:

and ever would be to him was a fling, a short term affair while he looked for a woman he could trust and respect.

It wasn't what she'd wanted, what she had desperately hoped for. But it was what she'd let herself in for by jumping into bed with him whenever he lifted a finger, and by agreeing to spend these few days with him...

If she had held back, though she wasn't in his league, things *might* have been different. She *might* have gained his respect.

But it was too late now to make him see her in a different light... Or was it? Surely it had to be worth a try?

As she sat silently, feeling as if her heart was being squeezed by a giant fist, he stroked a finger down her cheek.

When she looked up at him, her face defenceless, vulnerable, he remarked, 'If we're going to the Trocadero, perhaps we ought to get moving. Time's getting on and you know what New York traffic's like...'

As they climbed the stairs together, with a sideways glance he suggested enticingly, 'However, we can make time if you'd care to share a shower?'

Her pulses leapt at the thought but, resolved not to commit herself any further until she'd had a chance to think, to decide on her policy, she shook her head.

He looked at her, assessment in his glance, and as though reading what was behind the refusal he made no attempt to persuade her.

Instead, he said, 'Oh, well, I suppose it wouldn't do any harm to save a bit of excitement for later.'

The master bedroom where her small amount of luggage now reposed, was a most attractive room. It had primrose walls, a cream carpet, a king-sized bed, walk-in wardrobes and twin bathrooms tiled in peach. Joel disappeared into the far one and, as she began to unpack her case, she heard the shower start to run.

Just for an instant she was sorely tempted to change her mind and follow him in, but then she found herself wondering how many times he and Tara had shared a shower.

It was a sobering thought, and one which served to stiffen her resolve.

She found fresh panties, her dress, her fun-fur jacket and the necessary accessories, before stowing away the rest of her belongings in the nearest wardrobe, which she was cheered to find was empty.

Then, leaving her bracelet and her pearl studs on the dressing table, she went into the luxuriously fitted bathroom, with its off-white carpet and mirrored walls.

Fifteen minutes later, showered, dried and perfumed, she made up with care and took her newly washed hair up into a fashionable chignon, before putting on her panties and returning to the bedroom.

There was no sign of Joel and no sound from the other bathroom.

Having rolled on silk stockings and slipped her slim feet into high-heeled strappy sandals, she donned her black cocktail dress, the material moulding itself lovingly to her curves as she zipped up the close-fitting bodice and adjusted the spaghetti shoulder straps.

That done, she gave herself a critical glance in the nearest mirror and decided that while she looked no better then all right, she would do.

There had been no time to think about her course of action, but for the evening at least, she decided firmly, she would leave all her worries behind her and simply enjoy the chance to be with Joel.

Leaving the earrings where they were, she slipped the bracelet back on her wrist, gathered up her evening bag and jacket and closed the bedroom door behind her.

As she made her way down the stairs, her earlier half-formed thought that there was some flaw in Joel's explanation of why he'd kept the bracelet returned to chafe her.

He had said something like, 'On an impulse…I picked it up'

That was straightforward and believable.

But then, when pressed, he had added, 'You could call it safe-guarding my interests. If you didn't happen to wait for me at the Dundale Inn, at least I'd have an excuse to see you again…'

That was the part that wasn't logical.

Earlier he had assured her that after fetching his car he'd meant to return, and that only joining the rescue party had stopped him.

At the time he had taken her bracelet, he could have had no idea that he might *need* an excuse to see her again.

So why had he taken it? Why had he lied to her?

As Bethany reached the living room she heard Joel's voice and hesitated. Had he another visitor? Or had Tara returned for a second try?

After a moment it became clear that he was talking on the phone.

'It's of the utmost importance…' he was saying. 'I need the document ready to be signed by tomorrow afternoon…' Then, 'Yes… Yes… Exactly as I've outlined…'

Unwilling to interrupt what was obviously an important business call, she waited.

'Well, at the moment, as far as money and power goes, I'm the best bet. And, however you look at it, the organ grinder has got to be a better proposition than the monkey…

'Yes, Paul, I know it must seem drastic to you, and I admit it's taking a big risk, but I can't see any other way. And I assure you that whether it works or not it has its compensations…

'Yes, yes… If there's any way I can *make* it work, I'm prepared to stick with it…

'I can't rule it out. That's why I want to be sure I can't be ripped off…'

As she waited for the call to end, Bethany became aware of the housekeeper approaching and, unwilling to be found hovering outside the door, turned the knob and walked in.

Joel was standing by the window, the phone in his hand, looking devastatingly handsome in well-cut evening clothes.

As she put her bag and jacket on the couch he acknowledged her presence with a little smile, before ending the call with a brisk, 'Thanks, then, Paul. See you tomorrow afternoon.'

Replacing the phone, he turned to Bethany and, taking both her hands in his, let his eyes travel from her shining head to her slender silk-clad legs. Suddenly uncertain, she asked, 'Will I do?'

'You look wonderful.'

Though she knew he was exaggerating, she could tell he was quite happy with her appearance.

His voice casual, he added, 'But you could do with a necklace and some earrings to complete the picture.'

'I'm afraid I only brought my pearl studs and they don't really go with the bracelet.' Then, awkwardly, 'Joel, about the bracelet...'

'What about the bracelet?' he asked evenly.

'You said you'd taken it so that if I didn't happen to wait at the Dundale Inn you'd have an excuse to see me again...'

'That's what I said,' he agreed evenly.

'But you must have taken it before you knew you might need an excuse.'

His white teeth gleamed in a grin. 'Of course you're right.' Then, curiously, 'What stopped you calling me a liar at the time?'

'I half knew there was a flaw, that your explanation wasn't logical, but I didn't have chance to think it through. Why did you say what you did?' She was hurt; she could feel him laughing at her again.

He smiled wryly. 'Because, at that point, I didn't want to tell you the truth and it was the best explanation I could come up with on the spur of the moment. A poor best, I admit. That's why I changed the subject so hurriedly…'

'Now, about that necklace and earrings…'

Standing her ground, she pointed out, 'You still haven't told me why you lied.'

Without answering, he crossed to the far wall and opened a hinged picture to reveal a small safe.

Bethany watched him key in a number and a moment later the door swung open.

Reaching inside, he withdrew a blue leather jewel case and opened the lid. Taking out a necklace and a pair of long earrings, the intricate gold loops of each set with red stones, he told her, 'Because I wanted these to be a surprise.'

Her gaze going from the sparkling jewellery in his hand to the bracelet on her wrist, she said numbly, 'They look as if they match.'

'That's what I thought when I first saw the bracelet, only until then I'd understood that the stones in the earrings and necklace were rubies. When you told me the ones in the bracelet were garnets, I began to have doubts.

'I wanted to see the three pieces together before I said anything…'

Laying the items he was holding on the coffee table, he invited, 'Take a closer look.'

Filled with a kind of agitated excitement, her thoughts stampeding in all directions, she examined the pieces.

'What do you think?' he queried. 'Are they a set?'

'They appear to be.'

His face hard, he asked, 'How did you say you came by the bracelet?'

Completely thrown, wishing she could tell him the truth, but afraid of dropping Michael in it, she answered, 'Someone brought it into the shop.'

'Who?'

'Tony dealt with it.'

'But Feldon didn't want the bracelet so you bought it?'

'Yes.'

'And you don't remember anything about the seller?'

Hating to lie, even tacitly, she shook her head.

'Was it a man or a woman?'

'A man.'

'Feldon Antiques don't ask sellers for any proof of identity or ownership?' He raised a brow quizzically.

They always had when James Feldon had been alive, but she was convinced that Tony wasn't so scrupulous.

Carefully, she answered, 'It all depends.'

'On what?'

'On how valuable the item is. Or if we happen to know the seller.'

'In this case?'

'The bracelet alone wasn't really that valuable.'

'I see.'

After a moment the hardness disappeared from his face and he remarked, 'Well, now you have your set. Let's see how it looks on.'

As he picked up the necklace and moved behind her to clasp it round her neck, she began, 'But the necklace and the earrings aren't—'

'I want you to wear them.' Seeing she was about to argue, he said firmly, 'Wear them now to please me and we'll talk about it later.'

He touched his lips to the warmth of her nape, making her shiver. 'Tom will be outside with the car, and I don't know about you, but I'm getting hungry.'

Responding to his urging, she put on the glamorous drop earrings.

'Let me look at you.' Standing back a little, Joel gave her a critical appraisal. 'They provide the finishing touch. Now you look a million dollars.'

He smiled at her and, like magic, the tension lifted and her heart lightened.

As he helped her into her fun-fur jacket, she got a vivid mental picture of Tara swathed in mink.

As if picking up the thought, he asked, 'Would you like a mink?'

Shaking her head, she said, 'I've never liked real fur,' and caught his look of surprise.

'Most of the women I've met would kill to be dressed in mink.'

'And you approve of that sentiment?

'Not at all,' he said coolly. 'I've always considered that real fur looks better on animals.'

He put on his own coat and a few seconds later they were descending the front stairs to the waiting limousine.

The night was cold and clear. The sidewalks gleamed and the air had a frosty sparkle to it. Street lamps shone through the skeletal trees and a three-quarter moon was riding high in the indigo sky.

It was a perfect night for romance, Bethany found herself thinking.

As though echoing that sentiment, when Joel reached across to fasten her seat belt he brushed her cheek softly with his lips.

Her heart suddenly felt too big for her chest.

As soon as they were settled into the sleek car, it pulled out to join the stream of traffic that was flowing along Mulberry Street.

Bethany had always found New York vibrant and exciting, especially at night, but with Joel by her side it acquired an extra special magic.

Watching her face in the shifting light and shadow, he said, 'You look as if you enjoy New York as much as I do.'

'It was love at first sight,' she admitted.

'And for me.'

Eager to know more about him, she said, 'Tell me what it's like to live here.'

As they headed Uptown, he talked about his love of New York, of the simple, everyday things that made up his life. Manhattan's canyon-like streets lined with skyscrapers, the parks and open spaces, the theatres and museums, the restaurants and cafés, the little delicatessens and the bookstores.

He told her all about the old-fashioned shop in Little Italy that smelt of cheeses and savoury sausages, of wine and pickles and herbs and spices; the restaurant in Chinatown that served steaming *dim sum* and pots of jasmine tea…

Spoken with less enthusiasm, it might have sounded mundane, ordinary, but what made it extraordinary was the warmth, the sheer enjoyment of life, that emanated from every word.

It provided an insight into the man himself and she listened, enthralled. This was someone not in the least materialistic, someone who, even had he been poor, would still have known how to get the best out of life…

'Here we are.' Joel's voice broke into her thoughts and a second or two later they were drawing up at the kerb.

From the outside, the Trocadero appeared simple and understated, a sheer expanse of black glass with only its name in discreet gold letters.

A black and gold awning stretched across the sidewalk to where a man in black and gold livery was waiting to open the door.

As soon as they were inside the elegant black and white foyer, a man in immaculate evening dress came forward to greet them.

'Good evening, Mr McAlister, madam.'

They were relieved of their coats and led through to an inner foyer, where a double archway led to a spectacular black and white dining area with a central dance floor.

The *maître d'* was about to show them to their table when a female voice cried, 'Joel, darling! What luck!'

With a sinking heart, Bethany turned to see Tara, looking striking in an emerald-green dress and matching stole, standing close by. She was accompanied by a narrow-faced, effeminate-looking young man and a well-dressed older couple.

Taking Joel's arm possessively, she smiled up at him. 'You will join us, won't you…? He must join us, mustn't he, Daddy?' she appealed to the older man.

'Please do,' he returned civilly.

'Thank you,' Joel began politely, 'but, as you can see, I'm with—'

'Of course your little friend can come too,' Tara broke in condescendingly.

Ignoring her, Joel turned to address the older man, who was looking downright uncomfortable. 'It's very kind of you to invite us, sir,' he said smoothly. 'But we had planned on a romantic tête à tête.'

Turning to Bethany, he went on, 'May I introduce Sir William Lampton… Sir William, my fiancée, Bethany Seaton.'

Though she knew that Joel was only paying Tara back, Bethany felt as though she'd been kicked in the chest. Somehow she managed to summon a smile and murmur, 'How do you do?'

'Miss Seaton, how nice to meet you.' Taking her proffered hand, Sir William added gallantly, 'If you will allow me to say so, you look delightful…

'May I introduce my wife, Eleanor…? And Tara's friend, Carl Spencer…'

When the polite murmurs had subsided, without so much as a glance in Tara's direction, Joel said, 'Well, if you'll excuse us, I hope you all have an enjoyable evening.'

He put a hand at Bethany's waist and they followed the *maître d'*—who had been hovering at a discreet distance—through the nearest archway and into the dining area where, on a central dais, a small orchestra was playing softly.

Most of the widely spaced tables were already occupied by a well-dressed clientele ranging from the quietly wealthy to the downright ostentatious.

Perfume wafted, jewels glittered and champagne corks popped, while soft-footed waiters moved about and conversation and laughter mingled.

Led by the *maître d'* and followed by two of his minions, they were shown to a table adjoining the dance floor, where a bottle of vintage champagne was waiting in an ice bucket.

As soon as they were seated they were handed white leather menus with gold tassels to peruse, while the wine waiter eased off the champagne cork with a satisfying pop and poured the sparkling wine.

When their order had been given and they were alone, lifting his glass, Joel smiled at Bethany over the rim and toasted, 'To the most beautiful woman in the room.'

Flustered by what she saw as an over-the-top compliment, she said, 'I'm afraid that, compared to some women, I'm nondescript.'

'If you mean Tara, then not in my opinion,' he disagreed. 'Tara is blatantly beautiful, but you have a quiet, haunting loveliness that gets under a man's skin, a luminous, lit-from-within quality that lifts you into a different class.'

'But Tara is—'

'Tara is wilful and unkind,' he said dispassionately.

'I just wish you wouldn't use *me* to pay her back,' Bethany said quietly.

'You think that's what I was doing?'

She looked down at her hands in her lap. 'Wasn't it?'

'No.'

'Oh, I see… You were trying to salvage my pride. I suppose I should feel grateful, but—'

His voice smooth as silk, he told her, 'As I was doing nothing of the kind, there's really no need to feel grateful.'

For a moment she just stared at him before asking, 'Then what made you lie to Sir William?'

He clicked his tongue reprovingly. 'Now, do I look like a man who would lie to a baronet?'

Determinedly ignoring his levity, she said flatly, 'You told him I was your fiancée.'

'I don't regard that as lying, merely jumping the gun a little.'

'Jumping the gun?' she echoed blankly. 'I don't understand.'

'It's quite simple. If we go to Tiffany's tomorrow morning you can choose a ring…'

Her heart beginning to do strange things, she echoed, 'A ring?'

'An engagement ring.' Reaching across the table, he put a finger under her jaw and made a pretence of lifting it. 'Isn't that what couples who are planning to get married usually do?'

Wondering if this was some cruel joke, she said unsteadily, 'But we're not planning to get married.'

'Don't you want to marry me? Or are you just vexed because I haven't proposed in the good old-fashioned way? If it's the latter, then I'll see about rectifying matters later.'

'It's not… I mean…'

'You don't want to be my wife?'

She did. Oh, she did.

Unsteadily, she said, 'This idea of getting married… It's so sudden… So spur of the moment.'

'Not at all. I've had it in mind almost since we met… I told Henri you were my fiancée and we were planning to get married in New York…'

That accounted for the champagne and the change in the steward's manner, Bethany realized dazedly.

'And Molly believes we are,' Joel went on. 'Otherwise she would never have approved of us sharing a room…

'Ah, this appears to be our first course arriving, so I suggest we leave any further discussion until tomorrow and simply enjoy the rest of the evening.'

When the avocado starter had been placed in front of them and the waiter had retired, Joel changed the subject smoothly by asking, 'When were you last in New York?'

'A couple of months ago,' she answered abstractedly.

For the remainder of what proved to be an excellent meal— although afterwards Bethany could not remember what she'd eaten—he kept the conversation light and general.

Allowing herself to be swept along by the tide, she gave up all attempts to think and followed his lead.

When, their coffee finished, he took her hand and led her on to the dance floor, she went into his arms like someone coming home.

He held her close, his cheek against her hair, while for the next hour or so they danced every dance and, for Bethany at least, the time passed in a haze of pleasure.

Even the occasional glimpse of a sparkling Tara dancing with a series of young men failed to douse that pleasure.

After a particularly slow smoochy number, her head on Joel's shoulder, her eyes closed, Bethany was half asleep when he queried, 'Tired?'

'A bit,' she mumbled.

'As it will be the early hours of the morning in London, I suspect that's an understatement, so I suggest we leave before the cabaret starts.'

As though admitting she was tired had compounded that tiredness, she collected her evening bag and sleepwalked her way back to the foyer, where their coats appeared as if by magic.

A supporting arm around her, Joel escorted her out to the waiting limousine and settled her in. By the time he slid in beside her and drew her close, she was fast asleep.

When they reached the brownstone, she surfaced long enough to cross the sidewalk and, Joel's arm about her waist, climb the stairs on legs that felt like indiarubber.

Once in the hallway, Joel slipped her coat from her shoulders before helping her up the stairs and into the bathroom.

Lowering her on to a stool, he asked, 'Think you can manage now?'

She nodded and with fumbling fingers she cleaned her teeth and unpinned her hair...

It was broad daylight when she opened her eyes. She was alone in her bed. Only it wasn't her bed and, though her surroundings were attractive, the room was a strange one.

Her mind a blank, for a moment or two she couldn't think where she was.

Then it all came rushing back. She was in New York. In Joel's house. In Joel's bed. Though without the slightest notion of how she'd got there.

She was naked—apart from the necklace, earrings and bracelet she still wore—but with no recollection of taking off her clothes.

The last thing she could vaguely remember was leaving the Trocadero with Joel's supporting arm around her.

A lethal combination of champagne and jet lag must have suddenly caught up with her.

Frowning, she made an effort to think back, but now the whole evening seemed unreal, the focus shifting, the boundaries blurred. Had Joel really talked about marriage? Or was that just wishful thinking? Something she'd dreamt up…?

She jumped as, without warning, the door opened and Joel strolled in carrying a tray of tea.

Smartly dressed, his corn-coloured hair smoothly brushed, his silvery-green eyes bright, he looked the picture of health and vitality.

Smiling at her, he observed, 'So you're awake at last. How do you feel?'

Knocked sideways by that smile, she pushed herself upright and said huskily, 'Fine, thank you.'

His appreciative gaze on her bare breasts, he murmured, 'That's good.'

Blushing, she pulled up the duvet and trapped it under her arms. 'I don't remember getting undressed or going to bed.'

He put the tray on the cabinet and sat down on the edge of the mattress to pour the tea before he told her, 'I undressed you and put you to bed. You were absolutely shattered. Out on your feet.'

'Oh…' She blushed even harder.

Straight faced, he asked, 'Would it make you feel any better if I told you I kept my eyes closed?'

In no mood to be made fun of, she said crossly, 'No, it wouldn't.'

'Well, in that case I may as well admit that I enjoyed the scenery enormously.'

Then, unrepentantly, 'There's no need to look so *bothered*. I have seen you naked before.'

That was true enough. But somehow the fact that she hadn't been *conscious* made a difference.

Watching her face, reading her discomfort, he frowned. 'Before you put me down as a voyeur or a violator, my interest was healthy and wholesome and, apart from lifting you into bed, I never laid a finger on you.'

An edge to his voice, he added, 'Believe me, I like my women wide awake and cooperative.'

Instantly contrite, and upset because she'd angered him, she whispered, 'I'm sorry. I didn't mean to suggest...' Her smoke-grey eyes filled with tears. Unwilling to let him see them, she bent her head.

Putting a finger beneath her chin, he lifted it.

She blinked and a single bright tear escaped and began to trickle down her cheek.

He cursed himself for his brutish behaviour. Leaning forward, he caught it on the tip of his tongue. 'Don't cry, my darling,' he said softly. 'It's my fault. I was being offensive.'

Almost to himself, he added, 'I tend to think of you as being tougher than you are.'

He kissed her lightly on the lips and, handing her a cup and saucer, ordered gently, 'Now drink your tea.'

Her heart once again full to overflowing, she began to sip.

Studying the faint flush of sleep still lying along her high cheekbones and the dark silky hair tumbling round her shoulders, he sighed.

At her enquiring glance, he told her, 'You look so beautifully tousled and sexy. If you're not out of that bed pretty soon I may well give way to the temptation to rejoin you.'

Uncombed and unwashed, feeling anything but desirable, she was cheered by his words.

Reaching out a hand, he set one of the earrings swinging. 'Far from being nondescript, you look as exotic as Cleopatra in those and the necklace.'

'Why didn't you take them off?'

His even white teeth gleamed in a smile. 'I've always fancied sleeping in the same bed as Cleopatra.'

'How do you come to have them?' she asked cautiously.

'They were my mother's.'

'Oh…' Michael had told her that the bracelet had been his grandmother's.

'My father gave them to her as a wedding gift.'

Her voice not quite steady, Bethany asked, 'Was there a bracelet too?'

'There was originally,' Joel answered. 'The last time I saw my mother wear the set was after my father and his second wife had been killed in a road accident. She wore it when she came over to London for the funeral.'

Seeing Bethany's puzzled frown, he explained, 'My mother left my father and the family home and went back to the States when I was three years old.'

'So you were brought up in the States.'

He shook his head. 'She didn't take me. My mother had never wanted children and after my birth she suffered from depression. We saw virtually nothing of each other until I was grown up.'

There was a bleakness in his voice that—thinking of her own happy childhood—almost brought tears to Bethany's eyes. 'Oh, I'm sorry…' she whispered.

'Which goes to prove you have a kind heart,' he said derisively. 'But there's really no need to feel sorry for me. My grandmother was very fond of me and looked after me extremely well until I was seven.

'It was then my father met and married a young widow with a one-year-old baby…'

'Michael?'

'That's right.'

'So you had a real mother at last.' She smiled up at him with wide innocent eyes. Joel leant forward and tucked a stray tendril behind her ear.

'Unfortunately not. My stepmother didn't like me. I can't say I blame her. I was an awkward brat who fiercely resented her taking over my father's life.

'Finally she got fed up and told him either I went or she did…'

Her eyes on his face, Bethany waited.

After a moment he said bleakly, 'There was no contest. Despite my grandmother's objections—she thought I was too young—my father decided to send me away to boarding school.'

Sorry for the child who must have felt rejected by both of his parents, she put her hand on his.

For an instant he looked startled. Then he took her hand and gave it a squeeze. 'As I just said, you have a kind heart.'

This time there was no derision in the words.

CHAPTER SEVEN

AFTER a short pause, feeling the need to know, Bethany asked, 'So you went to boarding school?'

'For a few months, but I was so unhappy that I ran away. Needless to say, I was soon tracked down and taken home.' His laugh was cold.

'My father was furious and made arrangements to send me back. But this time my grandmother put her foot down and refused to let me go. Instead she suggested that my aunt and her husband, who had no children of their own, might have me for a while.

'They said they'd be happy to give it a try. Looking back, I don't think any of them really expected me to settle so far away from London…'

'Your aunt… did she live in Cumbria?'

'Got it in one. She and her husband have a farm in the Dundale Valley that's been in her husband's family for generations.'

Bethany urged him to continue. 'And you liked it there?'

'Loved it. Even when I was finally sent away to boarding school I regarded the farm as home and always went back there during the holidays. I still visit them regularly.'

So that explained his connection with the Lakes, and his knowledge of the fells…

Glancing at his watch, he said, 'I suggest we get moving. It's almost eleven and we've a busy day ahead.'

'Doing what?' she asked.

His voice casual, he told her, 'Visiting my solicitor, lunching in China Town—that is if you like Chinese food...?'

'I've never tried it,' she answered shyly.

'In that case you must certainly try it.' Then, with no change in tone, 'After lunch we'll go and choose a ring and if we're getting married tomorrow, as I'd planned—'

Bethany was shocked. 'But we can't possibly get married tomorrow.'

'Of course we can. All we have to do is go to the nearest city clerk and apply for a marriage licence, which we then sign in his presence. That's all there is to it.'

Not sure whether she was on her head or her heels, she said, 'Surely there's more to it than that?'

'Not in New York State. After a waiting period of twenty-four hours, the wedding can take place. All we need is someone in authority to actually perform the marriage ceremony.'

Though it was all her dreams and wishes realized and gift-wrapped, with a sudden, unreasonable feeling of panic she remembered the old warning, *Be careful what you wish for, it may come true.*

Watching her face, he said carefully, 'Of course there's one very important thing that still needs to be done.'

He took her hand and, raising it to his lips, dropped a kiss in the palm. 'Will you marry me?'

Her heart leapt wildly in her breast and for an instant she was tempted to say yes, to snatch at the happiness he seemed to be offering. But common sense stopped her.

Her throat desert dry, she said huskily, 'I don't understand why you want to marry me.'

His raffish smile melted her heart. 'Then you underrate your feminine charms.'

It was, in a way, a flattering answer. But as he was a man who, not only because of his wealth and position but because of his looks and charisma, could have his pick of beautiful women, it wasn't one she was prepared to accept at face value and she said so.

His eyes glinting between long, thick lashes, he said, 'In that case I'll put it even more simply. It's you I want in my bed.'

With a mixture of pain and pleasure and regret, she pointed out, 'I'm already there. You don't have to marry me.'

'I *want* to marry you.'

She still didn't believe him…couldn't let herself believe him. 'Why? Though my parents are decent people, I'm not from a wealthy background or—'

'As I've no intention of asking for a dowry—' he grinned '—I don't need anyone from a wealthy background.'

Her voice sounded meek as she continued. 'I don't really belong in your world—'

'Let me be the judge of that.' He lifted her chin so her gaze met his.

Trying to keep a level head despite the passion in his eyes, she said hesitantly, 'You don't really know me. I could be spiteful, mean-spirited, bad-tempered, awful to live with—'

'I don't believe you're any of those things,' he broke in calmly. 'And, as for not knowing you, when you're my wife, I'll get to know you.'

'But if you discover then that you've made a mistake, that you really don't like me, it will be too late. If we waited a while, got to know each other first…'

Joel frowned. After what he'd seen as a token hesitation the previous night, he had fully expected her to agree without further ado and this resistance surprised him.

Levelly, he said, 'I don't want to wait. Believe me, I'm not only used to making snap decisions, I'm used to those decisions being right.'

She sighed. 'But in business it's not such a big risk. If it happens to be the wrong decision it should be possible to rectify it. Marriage isn't like that…'

He raised an eyebrow. 'If you look at—'

'I know what you're going to say. That one in three couples get divorced, and that's one of the reasons I think it would be better to wait. It doesn't make sense to rush into it.'

Attacking from a different angle, he said, 'I take it you don't find me repulsive or you wouldn't be where you are now.'

'Of course I don't find you repulsive.'

He raised his eyebrow questioningly. 'Then what do I need to say to persuade you?'

All he needed to say was, I love you, but she could hardly tell him that.

Instead, she said, 'You're not in love with me.'

'*You're* not in love with me,' he countered. 'But that doesn't mean our marriage won't work.

'As far as marrying for love goes, I've known more than one marriage fail when the couple have been madly in love and then discovered that love alone isn't enough.

'The main thing is, I believe we're compatible in a lot of ways. We're on the same wavelength, the chemistry between us is fantastic…'

Leaning forward, he took her face between his palms. 'Let's give it a try.'

She wavered, *wanting* to, but held back by the knowledge that he didn't love her. Though if she agreed to marry him there was a chance he might come to care for her. While if she refused she could well have lost her one and only opportunity.

'Is the answer yes?' he pressed.

Knowing she couldn't turn down this prospect of happiness, she nodded, and heard his sigh of relief before his mouth covered hers.

As he kissed her, his hands moved across her shoulders and slid beneath the duvet until they reached the swell of her breasts.

When he had stroked and teased the nipples into firmness, his mouth left hers to pleasure first one and then the other, while his hand travelled over her flat stomach to the silky warmth of her inner thighs.

She was just abandoning herself to the pleasure, when he drew away and said reluctantly, 'We ought to be moving. We haven't much time. After we're married we'll be able to forget about everything else and concentrate exclusively on each other.' He grinned raffishly.

Hearing *after we're married* spoken so casually served to make the notion more real, and for the first time she was almost able to believe it.

Rising to his feet, suddenly businesslike, he said, 'While you shower and dress I've a couple of phone calls to make, then we can get started.'

For a little while after he'd gone she sat quite still, staring after him. It was only four days since they'd met, and so much had happened so quickly that she was starting to feel like a piece of tumbleweed caught and bowled along by the wind.

When she had taken off the jewellery and put it safely in the top drawer of the bedside cabinet, she cleaned her teeth and showered.

Then, dressed in a fine wool dress the colour of lilac and suede boots, she made her way downstairs to find Joel waiting in the hall.

Smiling at her, he said, 'I've had a word with a friend of mine, the Reverend John Daintree. He'll be happy to marry us at the Church of the Holy Shepherd at two o'clock tomorrow afternoon.'

'Oh…' She stopped abruptly and stood silently.

He looked at her steadily. 'Do you have a problem with that?'

'No… No. Only for some reason I'd expected a civil ceremony.'

His voice cool, he asked, 'Does that mean you would prefer one?'

'Not at all. I'd much prefer to get married in a church. It's just…' She bit her lower lip.

'Just what?' He pressed her to continue.

'I've always thought that a church wedding seems more *binding* somehow.'

'And you don't want that?'

'I wasn't totally sure *you* did.' She spoke the half-formed thought.

'I can assure you that, having decided on a wife, if at all possible I intend to stay married.'

Vastly relieved, she gave him a radiant smile.

'If you smile at me like that I'll forget all my good intentions and take you back to bed.'

'You said we hadn't much time,' she reminded him.

'Mmm…So I did. I'll just have to settle for a kiss then, won't I?'

She waited.

His hands on her hips, he lifted her on to her toes. 'Now *you* can kiss *me*.'

Just looking at his mouth made her heart beat faster and butterflies dance in her stomach.

Putting her hands on his shoulders, she touched her lips to that beautiful mouth and felt her heart start to thump against her chest bone.

He slanted his head, his lips parted, and he deepened the kiss until every nerve in her body came to life and her stomach clenched.

Fully aware of his effect on her, a very male smile of satisfaction curved his mouth before he said, 'We'd better get started or we'll never get everything done.'

As they reached the front door, a phone started to ring. When Bethany glanced at him, he shook his head decidedly. 'We'll leave it for Molly or the answering machine to pick up.'

The limousine was waiting by the kerb, with Tom standing by to open the door. He greeted them cheerfully. 'Morning, sir, madam… Lovely day, isn't it? Let's hope it stays like this. Where to first?'

As Bethany hadn't eaten any breakfast they went first to China Town for an early lunch at Joel's favourite restaurant, a small, simple place where the locals ate.

The *dim sum* he ordered were brought in a selection of bamboo steamers. They looked to Bethany like small white dumplings.

'What do you think?' he queried, when he'd watched her sample a couple. 'If you really don't like them, I'll ask for something else.'

She beamed at him. 'Oh, I do. They're delicious.'

'Then that's another thing we agree on.'

Lunch over, their next port of call was to the office of the city clerk where they duly applied for, and signed, a marriage licence.

From there he surprised her by taking her to Tiffany's to buy a ring. She was wondering why he'd chosen to take her to the famous Fifth Avenue store, rather than a quieter, more private venue, when she recalled their conversation that very first night.

As though reading her thoughts, he grinned and said, 'In view of what you told me, I thought you might find Tiffany's romantic.'

The moment they entered the jewellery department, Bethany was very conscious of the overt interest that Joel, with his tough good looks, his powerful physique and his well-tailored clothes, aroused.

While they looked at a wonderful selection of engagement rings, though Bethany herself received a few envious glances, she was well aware that the attention of most of the females there was firmly focused on him.

He obviously knew it too.

His little smile ironic and with a kind of quizzical self-mockery, he deliberately set out to play the part of an attentive fiancé.

When, between them, they had narrowed the choice of rings down to two—a wonderful glowing ruby and a magnificent diamond solitaire—she tried them both on again. And again. Before, dazzled and dazed, she was forced to admit, 'I really can't decide.'

Joel took the solitaire and, slipping it back on her finger, lifted her hand to admire it. Then, turning to the elegantly turned out sales lady, he told her casually, 'We'll take them both.'

Obviously unsure that she'd heard him correctly, she asked, 'Did you say both, sir?'

Coming to life, Bethany began in an agitated whisper, 'Oh, but I don't—'

'Both,' Joel broke in firmly. Then, to Bethany, 'The diamond for your engagement ring and the ruby to go with your set.'

'Please, Joel,' she begged desperately, 'I really don't need—'

He leaned down and kissed her lightly, stopping the protest. 'Call it your wedding present.'

Smothering a romantic sigh, the sales lady asked, 'Will there be anything else?'

'We'll need a wedding ring.'

Bethany felt a little pang of disappointment. She had been hoping against hope that he would say *two* wedding rings.

A selection of plain and chased rings in varying widths was produced and, after trying a couple on along with the solitaire, she chose a plain one, narrow and dainty.

As the sales lady began to assemble them ready to pack, Joel said, 'Just the wedding ring and the ruby, if you please. My fiancée will wear the diamond.'

A few minutes later, Bethany walked out of the store with Joel's hand at her waist and his ring on her finger. Her joy was slightly shadowed by regret that she hadn't been brave enough to suggest that he too had a ring.

'Where to now, sir?' the chauffeur asked as he held open the car door.

'Paul Rosco's office, please, Tom,' Joel answered.

When they reached the glass and concrete tower block that housed Joel's solicitor, thinking that he might prefer privacy, Bethany suggested that she could wait in the car.

'Not at all. I need you to be there.'

Puzzled, she asked, 'Why?'

As they crossed the marble-floored foyer and took the high-speed lift up to the sixty-fifth floor, he told her, 'Paul is drawing up a marriage contract for us both to sign.'

It sounded so cold-blooded that a chill ran down her spine. 'A marriage contract?'

Perhaps he heard the dismay in her voice because he said re-assuringly, 'I assure you, it's quite usual these days.'

When she continued to look unhappy, he added with the merest touch of impatience, 'I know it's practical rather than romantic, but a contract protects both our interests. It sets out clearly where each of us would stand if, by any chance, our marriage failed…'

Bethany fought back her tears; it all seemed so businesslike and unfeeling. When they reached the solicitor's offices, a smart young woman sitting at a computer in the outer office glanced up with a friendly smile that included them both. 'If you'd like to go on through, Mr McAlister, Mr Rosco is expecting you.'

Bethany had presumed that Paul Rosco's office would be all glass and chrome and sharp angles, but it was unexpectedly comfortable and welcoming with a thick pile carpet, a doe-coloured leather couch and a couple of deep armchairs.

A vase of fresh flowers stood on a side table and on a nearby bookcase there were several family photographs in silver frames.

Tall and dark, ruggedly good-looking, Paul Rosco came forward to greet them and the two men shook hands with real warmth.

An arm at Bethany's waist, Joel said, 'May I introduce my solicitor and good friend, Paul Rosco…? Paul, this is Bethany Seaton, my fiancée…'

'I'm very pleased to meet you.' Though the solicitor greeted her courteously, his expression was guarded, his blue eyes distinctly wary, as he shook her proffered hand.

'Won't you sit down?'

Feeling ill at ease, Bethany sat down on the soft leather couch.

'All set?' Joel queried, taking a seat by her side.

'All set,' Paul Rosco confirmed, producing a sheaf of legal-looking documents. 'I've laid it out exactly as you asked. All you have to do is each read through the contracts and agree to the contents before signing them.'

In silence she took the double page document she was handed.

Watching her face and noting that she wasn't happy, Paul Rosco began, 'I'm sure you'll find the suggested divorce settlement quite generous—'

'If you don't agree on the amount of support I've outlined,' Joel butted in, 'I'm quite willing to discuss it further.'

Wishing once again that he was a poor man and none of this was necessary, she said flatly, 'I don't want a divorce settlement. I don't need you to support me. If our marriage should break up, I'm quite capable of earning my own living.'

'It's not quite that simple,' Paul Rosco said carefully. 'For both your sakes you have to know exactly where you stand. If you haven't agreed on a settlement and the marriage does break up it could make things extremely difficult. Especially if there was any acrimony.'

She understood that he meant that Joel was a very wealthy man and, with no agreement, she could take him to court and try to fleece him. And, while she could vehemently deny that she would do any such thing, she knew that no one in their right senses would simply take her word. But a contract suggested that the man she loved didn't trust her. She felt belittled, humiliated.

Though why should he trust her? He didn't really know her any more than she knew him. She *might* be the kind of woman who would try to take a man for everything he had.

'And of course there's the question of children,' Paul went on blandly. 'If you were intending to have a family...'

Things had happened so quickly that she hadn't thought that far ahead, let alone discussed it with Joel. Now, chilled by uncertainty, she glanced at him, her grey eyes revealing how troubled she was.

He took her hand and squeezed it gently, a gesture that warmed her and made the situation seem more endurable. 'You do want children, don't you?'

'Yes,' she said in a small voice, and was rewarded with a smile that lifted her spirits even more.

'Then it would be wise to cover all eventualities, so I suggest that before you worry your head any more, you read the document.

'I've asked Paul to keep the whole thing simple and straight-forward, so it shouldn't take long to go through it.'

Realizing that if she wanted to marry Joel she had no choice, she began to read.

As the solicitor had said, the suggested divorce settlement was generous indeed, as were all the other maintenance commitments.

Telling herself that if the worst came to the worst and their marriage ended before they had a family, she could refuse Joel's money and simply walk away, she agreed to sign.

'Are you happy with it?' Joel pressed.

She nodded.

'Sure?' he asked quizzically. 'You look as if you're about to sign your own death warrant.'

'Quite sure.' Now the ordeal was over, she couldn't wait to put her signature to the document and have the whole thing over and done with.

'If you're both ready to sign, I'll ask Roz to come in and act as witness.' The solicitor touched a button and a moment later the girl from the outer office came hurrying in.

'So when is the wedding taking place?' Paul asked when both copies had been duly signed and witnessed.

'Two o'clock tomorrow afternoon at the Church of the Holy Shepherd. I was hoping you could spare the time to act as my best man.'

After the briefest of hesitations, Paul agreed. 'If you're sure that's what you want, I'll make time.'

The acceptance was courteous rather than enthusiastic, and Bethany felt sure he disapproved of such haste.

His manner, while scrupulously polite, hadn't really warmed towards her and, anxious to leave, she gathered up her bag, holding it against her chest like a bulletproof vest.

Apparently guessing how she felt, Joel declined Paul's offer of refreshments on the grounds that they still had things to do.

When they got outside the sun had gone down and it was clear and bitterly cold. Dusk and a myriad lights had magically combined to make a blue-velvet, jewel-encrusted evening cloak for the town to wear.

Bethany had presumed that Joel's statement that they still had things to do had simply been an excuse to get away. But when they were settled in the warmth and luxury of the limousine, he gave the chauffeur a strange address she didn't quite catch.

Unable to think of anything he had listed that morning that still needed to be done, she queried, 'Where are we going?'

'To buy you a wedding dress and a trousseau.' As her lips parted, he said, 'Don't argue. Tomorrow you'll be my wife…'

Tomorrow you'll be my wife… She was filled with a quiet happiness that dispelled the last of her lingering agitation, as he added firmly, 'And it's a husband's privilege to buy his wife's clothes.'

In the changing light she caught sight of a clock on the façade of a building that showed it was almost five o'clock. 'Isn't it a bit late to go shopping?' she ventured.

'Not to Joshua Dellon's. We're somewhat later than I'd hoped to be, but they're expecting us. I made all the arrangements this morning.'

When they drew up outside the famous fashion house, with its simple, yet stunning window displays, Bethany felt a stir of excitement.

She had always loved the flair and quiet elegance of Dellon's designs, but had never visualized herself in a position where she could afford to buy his exclusive creations.

As they crossed the sidewalk and approached the heavy smoked-glass door, it was opened by a stylishly dressed older woman with silver-blonde hair, who had obviously been watching out for them.

'Good evening.' She smiled at them both, adding, 'It's nice to see you, Mr McAlister.'

'It's good to see you, Berenice. I'm sorry we're a little late.'

She brushed aside his apology. 'That's quite all right. The traffic gets worse.'

'This is Miss Seaton, my fiancée.'

'Miss Seaton…' Berenice acknowledged the introduction gracefully.

Then, having passed her expert eye assessingly over Bethany, she turned to Joel and said, 'Miss Seaton has a beautifully proportioned figure and the size you suggested should fit perfectly.

'If there are any slight alterations needed I'll see that they're dealt with straight away. Now if you'll come through to the salon, everything's ready for you.'

The salon was palatial with rich carpets and sparkling chandeliers, rose-coloured velvet chairs and couches and polished woodwork..

There wasn't an article of clothing in sight.

A pair of chairs had been placed ready, and when Bethany was seated Joel sat down by her side. Though he appeared to be perfectly at ease, she thought how powerfully masculine he looked in such a very feminine setting.

As soon as they were seated, Berenice lifted a hand and at the given signal the dress show began.

For the next fifteen minutes a series of models paraded up and down, showing off coats and suits, day dresses and evening dresses, nightwear and lingerie.

While Devlin had been uninterested in what she wore, it soon became apparent to Bethany that Joel knew exactly what would suit her and how he wanted her to look.

From time to time, after an assessing glance in her direction, he'd nod, and Berenice would make a note in a small gold book with a gold pen.

In almost every case it was what Bethany would have chosen

for herself. The only thing she quibbled about was an evening dress with a fur wrap that he selected. And then not because of the dress itself, which was beautiful, but because it was clearly extremely expensive—even by Dellon's standards—and she felt he was spending quite enough.

'Of course you must have an evening dress,' Joel overrode her objection. 'And don't worry about the wrap,' he added. 'It may look like silver fox but it's not real fur, just dead teddy.'

'But I really don't need—' She protested.

'Oh, but you do. Tonight we're going to a very select twenty-first birthday party,' he went on ironically. 'A senator's daughter, no less… And I'd like to show you off.'

'Oh…' She wasn't at all sure she liked the idea of being 'shown off'. But, aware that if Joel was determined to take her to the party, she couldn't let him down by going in her inexpensive off-the-peg cocktail dress, she agreed meekly, 'Very well,' and the show went on.

The wedding gowns came last, glorious creations that would have made any bride look her best.

Joel sat back, one ankle crossed negligently over the other, and watched in silence while satin and lace, net and tulle swished and rustled past.

When the parade ended, Berenice gave him an enquiring glance.

'Can we see the first one again?'

'Of course.'

She snapped her fingers and the tall, slender, dark-haired model who had come on first, reappeared. The dress she was wearing was an ankle-length ivory sheath in wild silk, the way it was cut and the sheer beauty of the material making it look almost ethereal. With it was a short veil, fine as a spider's web, that was held in place by a simple coronet.

Glancing at Bethany, Joel asked, 'Do you like it?'

It was the one she would have chosen for herself and, pleasure and excitement making her sound breathless, she said, 'I love it.'

'Then we'll take it if it fits.'

As Berenice made a note in the gold book, a young woman brought in a still-smoking bottle of champagne and two crystal flutes.

After they had sipped the cool, sparkling wine and discussed shoe size and accessories, Berenice led Bethany away to try on the dress.

It fitted to perfection and she caught her breath as she saw herself in the long mirror, delighted that she would look beautiful for Joel.

Berenice nodded her approval. 'As that fits so well, everything else will,' she announced with certainty.

When they got back to a waiting Joel, she informed him, 'The evening dress and accessories are being packed and everything else will be delivered first thing in the morning.'

Just as she finished speaking, an elegant black box with the name Joshua Dellon in gold script, was carried in and handed over.

They thanked Berenice and, looking well pleased, she escorted them to the door and bade them a courteous, 'Goodnight.'

The limousine appeared as if by magic and, as soon as they were settled in, Tom started for home.

It had been a day full to overflowing and Bethany felt like pinching herself to prove that she wasn't dreaming. Instead she looked at the magnificent diamond on her finger that picked up every stray gleam of light and thought how lucky she was.

But, even as the thought crossed her mind, she knew that, had she the chance, she would give up the ring and everything she owned in exchange for Joel's love.

Glancing sideways at him, she saw the gleam of his eyes and realized he was watching her.

'Penny for them,' he offered.

'I was just thinking how lucky I am.'

His mouth seemed to tighten and, feeling as if she was in a lift that was dropping too fast, she wondered what she'd said to annoy him. But a split second later that tautness was gone and she knew it must have been a trick of the light.

Taking her hand, he raised it to his lips. 'Not at all. I'm the lucky one to win you for a wife…'

Though she was thrilled by his words, she was wondering for the umpteenth time why, when he didn't love her, he was so set on marrying her, when he added, 'You could have chosen to marry Michael.'

The mention of Michael, and the thought of hurting him, cast a shadow over her happiness. 'I really must talk to him and tell him the truth.' Guiltily, she added, 'I've treated him very badly.'

'I agree that we need to talk to him, but I suggest that we leave it until after we're married. Better to present him with a *fait accompli*. That way, instead of arguing, he'll be forced to accept the situation.'

But would he accept it? Or would it cause trouble between the two men? Unconsciously she sighed.

Joel put an arm around her and drew her close. When his lips sought and found hers, she wondered briefly if he was kissing her to take her mind off Michael.

Then he deepened the kiss and she could think of nothing but him. The best of companions, the sweetest of lovers, the man she adored and hoped to spend the rest of her life with.

CHAPTER EIGHT

WHEN THEY ARRIVED at Mulberry Street, Joel gathered up Dellon's black and gold box and helped Bethany out. Who said you could never see stars in New York? she thought as, held securely in the crook of his arm, leaning a little against him, she looked up at the star-spangled sky.

'Will you be wanting me again tonight, sir?' the chauffeur asked.

Joel shook his head. 'No, you've had a full day. Put the car away and take the evening off. We'll get a taxi.'

'Thank you, sir,' Tom said gratefully. 'Goodnight, sir. Goodnight, madam.'

As Joel opened the front door, the housekeeper came into the hall. 'Oh, Mr McAlister, young Mr Michael's been trying to get through to you all afternoon. He asked me to ask you to ring him as soon as you got back. He says it's absolutely essential that he speaks to you.'

'Thank you, Molly,' Joel said easily. 'I'll take care of it.'

'Will you be wanting a meal tonight?'

'No, we'll be going out. You and Tom can relax.'

She smiled her thanks and left them alone.

With his arm around Bethany's waist, Joel shepherded her towards the stairs.

When they reached their bedroom, feeling anything but easy, she began, 'Perhaps I'd better talk to Michael after all—'

'We're due at the party in less than an hour,' Joel pointed out evenly, as he put the black and gold box on the bed. 'There's no time tonight to make explanations or listen to what will no doubt be long, impassioned appeals.'

'I expect you're right.' Not looking forward to talking to Michael, Bethany was cravenly pleased to put it off.

Determinedly changing the subject, Joel said, 'Red stones won't go with your dress so I thought you might care to wear these.' As he spoke he crossed to a bow-fronted chest and, unlocking one of the top drawers, took out a small case and handed it to her. She opened the lid to find a pair of earrings, each made up of a single long strand of diamonds that sparkled and glittered in the light.

'They're lovely,' she breathed.

'I'm glad you like them.'

Before she could even thank him, he added, 'Now I've a couple of things to do and some emails to read before I shower, so I'll leave you to get on.'

He made no mention of showering together, as he had done the previous night, and she didn't know whether to be pleased or sorry.

But, considering they hadn't a great deal of time, it was perhaps as well, she told herself sternly as she put the case on the bed and began to unpack her new finery.

Lifting the dress carefully from its cocoon of fine black tissue paper, she found herself thinking that she had never before owned anything so lovely.

It was midnight-blue and made of shimmering silk chiffon, with a daringly-cut bodice and a skirt that swooped from just below knee-length at the front to a long, graceful fish-tail at the back.

Packed with it were a matching bra and briefs, sheer silk

stockings, evening sandals in her size, a small purse with a silver wrist chain and the soft, man-made fur wrap.

Leaving them all laid out on the bed, she took off her ring and went to shower.

She emerged some twenty minutes later, powdered and perfumed and lightly made-up, her long dark hair taken up into a smooth, elegant chignon that showed the pure line of her throat and jaw.

There was no sign of Joel.

Taking off her dressing gown, she put on the delicate underwear and the sheer silk stockings and shoes, before replacing her ring and fastening the earrings to her neat lobes.

Then, feeling a kind of awe, she slipped into the dress. Like gossamer against her skin, it settled into place, clinging lovingly to her slender curves. The bodice was a little lower-cut than she usually wore and she hoped there wasn't too much cleavage showing as, holding her breath, she looked in the long mirror.

She was still gazing speechlessly at the beautiful stranger who stood gazing back at her, when Joel appeared behind her, looking devastatingly handsome in an immaculate evening suit.

He was freshly shaven and his thick corn-coloured hair was making efforts to curl a little against his well-shaped head.

His hands lightly on her shoulders, he turned her round and, holding her at arm's length, studied her in silence.

After what seemed an age, he said huskily, 'You look enchanting. Every man there will envy me and I'll be madly jealous of every man who dares to look at you.'

A catch in her voice, she pointed out, 'You said you wanted to show me off.'

'Now I'm not so sure. I don't want a lot of strange men feasting their eyes on you. I'm beginning to see why some cultures prefer to keep their women veiled.' His eyes fixed on her mouth, he asked, 'Will it do irreparable damage to your lip-gloss if I kiss you?'

By way of answer, she lifted her face like a flower to the sun.

He kissed her lightly, but with a sweet thoroughness that brought a faint flush to her cheeks and enough warmth to the rest of her body to make her wish they weren't going out.

When he reluctantly lifted his head, she opened her eyes and saw by the expression on his face that he was wishing much the same.

'Do we have to go?' she asked impulsively.

'I'm afraid so. I promised Lisa.'

Bethany's heart sank. It had been Lisa's party that Tara had asked Joel to take her to, although she already had an escort.

'Tara will be going.' She spoke the thought aloud.

'Does that bother you?'

Lifting her chin, she lied, 'Not really.'

Not taken in for a moment, he said, 'Don't worry, with so many people present, we might never even set eyes on her…'

I do hope so, Bethany thought, and it was almost like a prayer.

'And I'll be there with you. Though I must admit I'd much sooner be here alone with you.'

Sighing, he added, 'However, I'll console myself with the thought that if we so desire we can spend our entire honeymoon in bed.'

'Are we having a honeymoon?'

'I thought a few days in the Catskills. I've a cabin there.' A shadow crossed his face as he added, 'Then there's something I have to take care of. Though, hopefully, when everything's finally resolved, we can have another honeymoon anywhere you fancy.

'Now, about ready? The taxi should be here.'

When she had dropped one or two things into her evening purse, he put the fur wrap around her shoulders and escorted her down the stairs to the waiting taxi.

The party was being held at the Cardinal, Joel told her as they headed Uptown. Rated as one of the oldest of New York's top hotels, it was also one of the smallest. Yet it was almost an institution, with all the cachet to make it select and sought after.

He went on to say that with money no object—the Senator came from a very wealthy and privileged background—the entire hotel had been taken over for the party and the many distinguished guests who were staying the night.

Wondering afresh if she would fit into his world and starting to feel newly anxious at the prospect of the coming evening, Bethany found herself praying that she wouldn't let Joel down.

Watching her face in the changing light, he asked, 'You're not nervous, are you?'

'A bit,' she admitted.

He squeezed her hand. 'There's no need to be, I assure you. You speak well and look great and, unlike some of the empty-headed socialites I know, you're intelligent and articulate.'

Somewhat cheered by his praise, she made an effort to stop worrying about the coming evening, though the possibility of running into Tara still lingered like a shadowy threat at the back of her mind.

They found the traffic was heavy and by the time their taxi drew on to the hotel's forecourt, the proceedings appeared to be well under way.

Inside the sumptuous foyer, Bethany was handed a cloakroom ticket and her wrap was whisked away. Then one of the many circulating waiters offered them a choice of champagne or freshly squeezed orange juice and a wonderful selection of tiny canapés.

They both refused the canapés, but Bethany accepted a glass of orange juice and Joel a glass of champagne. 'Ready for the fray?' he asked.

'As ready as I'll ever be,' she admitted wryly, and they made their way inside.

The party spread over three rooms—a long, elegant salon, a spacious supper room where a magnificent buffet was laid out and the chandelier-hung ballroom, where a small orchestra was playing softly.

Distinguished-looking men and beautifully dressed, bejewelled women were gathered in little groups laughing and talking.

The atmosphere was redolent of wealth and breeding and, though she was well aware that she didn't belong in that class, dressed as she was, Joel's arm at her waist and his words of praise still echoing in her head, she suddenly felt almost confident.

Their hostess, her father by her side, was waiting to greet them. It was immediately obvious that Senator Harvey, a tall, heavily built, balding man, liked the limelight, while his daughter didn't.

She was a pretty fair-haired girl, shy and mild-mannered who, though she was extremely well-dressed, seemed to be eclipsed by her august parent, if not by the occasion itself.

Her face lit up at the sight of Joel and Bethany found herself wondering if Lisa wasn't more than a little in love with him.

Holding out her hand, she told him breathlessly, 'When Tara said you were still in England, I'd begun to think you'd forgotten your promise.'

Taking the proffered hand, he raised it to his lips. 'Not at all. I wouldn't have missed your party for worlds.'

She flushed with pleasure.

'May I introduce my fiancée, Bethany Seaton…'

Some of the pleasure faded.

'Bethany, this is Lisa Harvey.'

Feeling sorry for the girl, Bethany murmured a pleasant greeting, which was returned.

Then, with a great deal more grace than Tara had shown, Lisa managed to smile and say, 'I'm so pleased you could come.'

Indicating the man by her side, she added, 'I'd like you to meet my father…'

Taking Bethany's hand, he said, 'It's nice to meet you, my dear.' He added gallantly, 'You look absolutely delightful.'

'Thank you,' she said demurely.

Still holding her hand, he asked, 'Dare I hope that later you'll dance with me?'

Knowing it was expected of her, she agreed. 'I'd love to.'

He glanced at Joel. 'Then all I need is your fiancé's permission.'

'You have it,' Joel said at once, 'so long as I can dance with your charming daughter.'

Looking looked both delighted and flustered, Lisa said breathlessly, 'Of course. Though I don't dance very well.'

Her father gave her a swift, irritated look that spoke volumes and made her soft mouth tighten.

Feeling sorry for the girl once more, Bethany said swiftly, 'I don't dance very well either, but I didn't have the courage to admit it, so I was going to let your father find out for himself.'

Some of the tension left Lisa's fair, wholesome, girl-next-door face and she smiled.

'Having danced with each of you ladies—' Joel entered the conversation '—I'm fully aware that you're both being far too modest.'

'Though it's not really the occasion for business,' the Senator remarked to Joel, 'I'd like a private word with you later, if Bethany—may I call you Bethany?—doesn't mind sparing you for ten minutes or so?'

'I certainly don't mind,' she agreed pleasantly and, in order to cover her initial slight hesitation, smiled at him.

'My dear,' he said, 'if you smile at me like that, you'll make me your slave for life.'

Greatly daring, she said, 'I think it would take more than a smile to enslave a man like you.'

Chuckling at her reply, he gave Joel a hearty slap on the shoulder. 'Joel, you old son of a gun, you're a very lucky man.'

Joel's dark gaze remaining on his fiancée, he smiled. 'Don't I know it.'

After some further conversation, when some late arrivals came they moved away to 'circulate and enjoy the party' as instructed.

For a while they drifted from group to group sipping their drinks, while Bethany was introduced to quite a number of Joel's personal friends as well as some of his business acquaintances.

To her very great relief there was no sign of Tara, and everyone she met was most pleasant and friendly. But when one young man, after goggling at her, tried to turn the conversation into personal channels, Joel put a masterful arm around her and whisked her off to the dance floor.

As they went into a slow dance, his cheek against her hair, he muttered, 'If that young oaf hadn't taken his eyes off you when he did, it would have been pistols at dawn.'

Feeling secretly a little thrilled by his proprietary manner, she half shook her head. 'He might have been young and a bit wet behind the ears, but there was no harm in him.'

'You have a kind heart,' Joel told her. 'I noticed it earlier when you lied to Lisa about not being a good dancer.'

'I know it sounds silly,' Bethany said a shade apologetically, 'but I felt sorry for her.'

'It's not silly. On the surface, Lisa has everything, but in reality she's just a poor little rich girl. She spends most of her time trying to please her father and failing. He's been trying to turn her into a society butterfly so she can marry a real go-getter.

'But, in my opinion, she would be a great deal happier married to a man who would appreciate her just as she is.'

As they finished their dance the Senator came up, his daughter on his arm, to claim his dance.

The next number was a quickstep and, seeing Lisa's anxious look, Joel suggested casually, 'As I've been out of town for a while, shall we have a drink before we dance and catch up on the latest gossip?'

She nodded gratefully.

Though a shade on the heavy side and without Joel's masculine grace, the Senator proved to be a good, if slightly flamboyant, dancer.

They had circled the floor before he remarked with just a suggestion of relief, 'My dear, you underrate yourself. You're a very good dancer.'

'Why, thank you,' she said demurely. Then so he wouldn't realize she'd lied, 'But I find it all depends on my partner. You're so easy to follow.'

Obviously pleased by her reply, he said, 'Judging by your accent, you're from England?'

'Yes. I live in London.'

'Lisa spent a year at St Elphins, which was reputed to be one of the best finishing schools in England. But, unfortunately, it didn't give her much in the way of social graces...'

Having a beautiful partner who was also a good dancer and listener suited the Senator very well and, as he seemed loath to give her up, they danced several dances.

Then the band began to play a modern waltz and Joel and Lisa joined them on the floor. Thanks to Joel's care, Lisa made a good showing and, happy to see it, Bethany remarked, 'Your daughter dances well.'

'Lisa's never been able to sell herself. She always comes over as shy and awkward.'

'I think you underrate her,' Bethany said firmly.

As soon as the waltz came to an end, though it was obvious that Lisa—flushed with success—would have liked to have stayed on the floor, Senator Harvey commandeered Joel.

'I'd like to have that word now, Joel, my boy, if the ladies will excuse us?'

Knowing there was nothing else for it, both women murmured assent and, the Senator's arm around Joel's shoulders, the men walked away.

Seeing that Lisa looked suddenly lost, Bethany suggested, 'I thought I might take this chance to slip off to the Ladies' Room and check my make-up.'

'I'll go with you,' the other girl responded with undisguised eagerness.

As they made their way back to the foyer, in a burst of confidence she said, 'Knowing he'd be busy at least part of the time, Daddy press-ganged Martin into being my escort, but I've hardly caught a glimpse of him so far.'

Then, with a flash of spirit, 'And I've no intention of going looking for him. Would you?'

'No, I wouldn't,' Bethany said. 'There must be nicer, more attentive men around.'

'David would have been happy to have escorted me,' Lisa went on, her blue eyes wistful, 'but he's only a junior partner in a struggling law firm and Daddy doesn't think he's good enough for me.'

Remembering what Joel had said, Bethany remarked quietly, 'Shouldn't it depend on what *you* think?'

Lisa gave her a thoughtful glance. 'Yes, it should, shouldn't it?

'We're not in love, or anything like that,' she added after a moment, 'but he does seem to like me, and he doesn't make me nervous like some of Daddy's friends do.'

The Ladies' Room was frankly luxurious. It was decorated

in rose and old gold and had soft lighting and a deep pile ivory carpet. Opposite a long dressing-table with gilt mirrors and vel-vet-covered stools, were several cushioned chairs and couches. Through an archway, Bethany glimpsed a row of gleaming wash-basins with gold-plated taps.

There were three beautifully dressed, sophisticated-looking women already there, chatting together in a little clique.

Ignoring Bethany, they gave the Senator's daughter smiles that held a combination of respect and envy and murmured how much they were enjoying the party.

After a moment or two, Lisa went through to wash her hands, while the women remained where they were. Conscious of their covert glances, Bethany took a seat on one of the stools and made a pretence of fixing her make-up.

Their conversation became *sotto voce* and, feeling a lot less confident without Joel's support, she was wondering uneasily if they were discussing her, when the door opened and through the mirror she saw Tara, resplendent in gold lamé, walk in.

'Well, well, well, look who's here!' she exclaimed. 'Joel's little friend. Where is he, by the way? Don't tell me he's abandoned you?'

Turning to face her, Bethany said evenly, 'He's talking to Senator Harvey.'

Eyeing Bethany's dress, Tara remarked, 'That looks like a Dellon... I presume Joel's taken you shopping. Payment for services rendered, no doubt.'

Her speech was slightly slurred and, judging by the glitter in her eyes and the flush lying along her cheekbones, she had drunk rather more champagne than was good for her.

Bethany bit her inner lip and said nothing.

'And diamond earrings too!' Tara went on shrilly. Then, with added venom, 'You must think you're on to a good thing—'

Bethany, very aware of the other women who were now staring openly, gathered up her bag and headed for the door.

Tara barred her way. 'But don't make any mistake about it, Joel's only using you to get his own back on me. A week or two at the most and you'll be out on your ear—'

Catching sight of Bethany's ring, she abruptly stopped speaking and simply gaped.

Then, rallying somewhat, 'You may be wearing a ring, but don't imagine for a moment that he seriously intends to tie himself to a little nobody like you. When it comes to actually applying for a marriage licence you'll find—'

'As a matter of fact we applied for a licence today,' Bethany said clearly, 'and we're getting married tomorrow afternoon.'

Her face twisted with rage, Tara hissed, 'Joel must be mad to marry a scheming little bitch he's only known a few days and who's been having it off with his stepbrother.

'Oh, yes, I know all about you and Michael. He got a nasty shock when I happened to mention your name. Until then he had no idea that you'd dumped him to go to New York with Joel…'

So Michael knew she was here…

'But then he should have had the sense to know that women like you always plump for the highest bidder…

'Well, if Joel is fool enough to marry you, don't think you've got it made. You'll never be accepted in good society, and it won't be pleasant to find yourself ostracised…'

Lisa, who had been standing silently in the background, moved forward and, slipping an arm through Bethany's, said, 'Come on, Bethany, we'd better be getting back.' As she brushed past Tara, adding, 'Lord Peter will be wondering where we've got to,' Bethany caught a glimpse of the other women's faces, all aghast.

When they reached the door, Lisa said in a stage whisper, 'I only hope you didn't take any notice of poor Tara. A combination of jealousy and too much champagne must have made her tongue run away with her.'

As soon as they were out of earshot, Bethany, her legs feeling oddly shaky, said, 'I can't thank you enough. You were great.'

Lisa giggled. 'I was rather good, wasn't I? To be honest, I surprised myself.' Then, more seriously, 'Don't let Tara upset you. She can be a cat at times, but she's usually sorry afterwards.'

Doubting that, Bethany said nothing.

'Now, just in case they keep an eye on us,' Lisa continued almost gaily, 'let's go and talk to Peter.'

Thinking of Michael and trying to push the guilt she felt to the back of her mind, Bethany asked, 'Is this Peter really a lord?'

'Oh, yes, though he doesn't use his title. His elder brother is the Duke of Dunway.'

Bethany giggled. 'I thought you might have made him up.'

'I'm afraid I'm not that resourceful. I met him when I was at finishing school in England. I was friends with his sister, Sarah.'

'Does he live in New York?'

Lisa shook her head. 'He lives on the family estate in Surrey, but he came over specially for my birthday…'

Bethany wondered how, when Lisa had such good friends amongst the aristocracy, the Senator could belittle his daughter's social graces.

After Bethany had been introduced to Lord Peter, a tall, fair, innocuous-looking young man with a nice smile and a cut-glass accent, he said, 'So you're English too?'

'Yes.' She smiled politely.

'Whereabouts do you live?'

Bethany took another orange juice from a passing waiter, and replied. 'London.'

'Are you London born and bred?'

She shook her head. 'I was born in Youldon.'

'Ah,' he sighed. 'Not far from the ancestral home. It's a real pain, nowadays, for seven months of the year it draws crowds of visitors, while the family live in what used to be the stables.'

'The old order changeth,' Bethany quoted.

'Too true,' he agreed. 'These days it's money that impresses people. Not blue blood or titles.'

With a glance at Lisa, Bethany murmured, 'Oh, I don't know.'

When Lisa, who seemed to sparkle in his company, admitted that she had used his title to impress, he threw back his head and laughed.

He was still laughing when Joel appeared out of the crowd and, putting an arm around Bethany's waist, said, 'I was starting to wonder where you'd got to.'

Introductions over, they stood chatting for a few minutes before going through to the supper room to eat, listen to the toasts and watch Lisa—her father by her side—cut the cake.

When Peter excused himself and moved away to have a word with someone he knew, Bethany said to Joel in an agitated whisper, 'I *should* have talked to Michael. He knows I'm in New York with you.'

His grip on her waist tightened. 'Are you sure?'

'Quite sure.' She nodded anxiously.

Joel's beautiful mouth tightened perceptibly. 'How does he know?'

'Apparently Tara mentioned my name to him.'

'I might have expected it,' he said grimly. 'I know they talk to each other on a regular basis.' Then, sharply, 'What else has she been saying to you?'

Bethany gave him a quick edited version of what had happened in the Ladies' Room.

Frowning, he said, 'Try not to let her spitefulness bother you. And don't fret about Michael. Though I would have much preferred to break the news myself, he had to know some time.'

'But I—'

Putting a finger to her lips to stop the words, he said, 'Don't worry. We'll talk to him tomorrow.'

Feeling bad about it, she pleaded, 'Couldn't we talk to him now?'

'I think not. For one thing, it'll be the middle of the night in London.'

Of course he was right. But how could he take the whole thing so *calmly*? she wondered.

The rest of the evening would have been enjoyable if the guilt she felt towards Michael hadn't hovered like a dark shadow at the back of her mind. As it was, she was pleased when, in the early hours of the morning, the party began to break up.

As they went to thank Lisa and her father and say their fare-wells, she asked Bethany in a whisper, 'Are you really getting married tomorrow…?'

'We are indeed,' Joel answered.

Looking uncomfortable, Lisa went on, 'Only Tara said you'd only known each other a few days…'

'It was love at first sight,' Joel told her. 'On my part, at least…'

If only that were true, Bethany thought wistfully. If it had been, despite all the problems caused by her association with Michael, she would have counted herself as one of the happiest girls in the world.

'So I'm afraid I rather swept Bethany off her feet,' Joel added with a smile.

'How romantic.' Lisa sighed deeply. 'I've always loved wed-dings.'

Acting on an impulse, Bethany began, 'Are you by any chance…?'

Suddenly remembering that the other girl might have a crush on Joel, and uncertain whether or not she was doing the right thing, she paused, wishing she'd kept her mouth shut.

Then, glancing at Joel, she caught his little nod of encouragement and, her heart lifting that they were so close that he often knew what she was thinking, she began again. 'Are you by any chance free tomorrow?'

'I am until early evening,' Lisa said. 'Then David is taking me to a special charity ball game. Why do you ask?'

A shade diffidently, Bethany explained. 'As I have no friends in New York, I was wondering if you might like to…'

As she hesitated, Lisa asked excitedly, 'Help you get ready? Of course I will.'

'We were thinking of a little more than that,' Joel put in. 'We were hoping you'd be a bridesmaid.'

'A bridesmaid…?' Lisa breathed. Then, colouring with pleasure, 'I'd love to.'

'It's only a quiet affair,' Bethany added.

'I'm sure it'll be wonderful.'

Smiling at her glowing face, Joel went on, 'You'll need a dress and all the trimmings, so can you be ready to go shopping by nine o'clock… say nine-thirty at the latest?'

At Lisa's eager nod, he went on. 'In that case I'll pick you up from home.'

Realizing too late that they had virtually ignored Lisa's father, Bethany made an effort to retrieve the situation. Turning to him with a brilliant smile, she said, 'I do hope you'll be able to come…'

'I'd certainly like to, my dear,' the Senator said. 'The only trouble is that I have to be at the airport by four-thirty.'

'That would be fine. The ceremony is at two o'clock at the Church of the Holy Shepherd,' Joel told him.

He smiled warmly at the couple. 'Then I'd love to attend.'

'Again we were thinking of something more than that,' Joel said. Then, in answer to the Senator's questioning glance, 'Though it's extremely short notice, we were rather hoping you would give the bride away.'

All at once Bethany's stomach knotted, as though his words were stones he'd hit her with.

'I'd be delighted, my boy,' Senator Harvey said heartily. 'Fill me in on the details tomorrow morning when you pick Lisa up.'

'I'll do that,' Joel responded.

As soon as he and Bethany had reiterated their thanks and said their goodnights, they made their way into the foyer, where she handed her cloakroom ticket to a hovering attendant.

'You look upset,' Joel said the moment they were alone. 'What's wrong?'

When, unable to speak for the lump in her throat, she stayed silent, he pressed, 'Do you have a problem with Lisa's father giving you away? If you do I'll—'

She shook her head. 'No, it's not that...'

'Then what is it?'

Her voice just a thread of sound, she said, 'I suddenly realized I'm getting married tomorrow and my mother and father don't even know.'

'And you're close to your parents?'

She nodded. 'Very.'

A frown drew Joel's well-marked brows together. 'Of course it's entirely my fault for rushing you so.'

His frown deepening, he added, 'Unfortunately, the jet's on this side of the pond, so it would mean them catching an ordinary flight, which would—'

She half shook her head. 'They wouldn't come anyway. Dad has a heart condition that makes him unable to fly, and Mum wouldn't come without him. It's just that I should have phoned them...'

Glancing at his watch, Joel said, 'Well, if you want to get them out of bed…?'

She shook her head. 'No, no… I'll talk to them in the morning.'

Feeling happier now, she smiled at him.

In return he squeezed her hand.

At that moment the attendant reappeared with Bethany's wrap and handed it to Joel, who put it around her shoulders.

Then, a hand at her waist, he escorted her through the handsome doors and out into the cold night air. The party, with its highs and lows, was over.

CHAPTER NINE

Outside the air seemed curiously still and a few flakes of snow were starting to drift down. After the warmth of the hotel it felt bitter and Bethany shivered as, amidst the departing bustle, Joel hurried her towards the waiting cab.

Just as they reached it there was a little flurry of footsteps, then Tara was by his side, clutching his arm. 'Joel, wait... I *have* to talk to you...'

Shaking off her hand, he opened the cab door and said to Bethany, 'Get in out of the cold.'

She obeyed and, as he closed the door behind her, he asked Tara coldly, 'What is it?'

Unwilling to be a spectator at what she felt sure would be an unpleasant little scene, Bethany turned her head away but she could still hear what was being said.

'Please, Joel,' Tara begged, 'tell me you have no intention of getting married tomorrow.'

'I have every intention of getting married tomorrow.'

He turned away to open the cab door but, catching his arm once more, she rushed on, 'I would have thought someone like you would find it too degrading to share a woman with another man... Especially his own stepbrother...'

'As a matter of fact I do, that's why I ended *our* relationship.'

'And that's what all this is about, isn't it?' Tara cried shrilly. 'If you hadn't caught Michael and me together and got angry, none of this would have happened. I believe you're just trying to get your own back and punish us both.'

He laughed coldly. 'If I was, could you blame me?'

'I don't know why you can't forget the whole thing. I told you it was just a one off, nothing serious. It would never have happened if we hadn't both been stoned out of our minds…'

'It's you I love, which is more than *she* does. Surely you can see she's just a common little slut who's on the make…'

'Watch your tongue,' Joel warned curtly.

'Well, she *is* a slut,' Tara insisted. 'Michael told me how she tried her wiles on him first and managed to get him to propose to her. But then, as soon as she realized you were a better bet, she dumped him and turned her attention to you…' Tara turned to stare at Bethany.

'Oh, she's clever, there's no doubt about it. Somehow she's managed to get Lisa eating out of her hand…'

Then, with a kind of helpless fury, 'When I asked Lisa why she'd stuck up for the scheming little bitch, she said, "I like her, she's been kind to me". *Kind…*'

Joel smiled grimly. 'Kindness is an attractive quality; you should try it some time.'

Tara was furious. 'How can you say—'

But Joel continued before she had a choice to finish. 'Bethany has a warm, spontaneous kindness that comes from a generous spirit, something you would know little about, Tara.'

Leaving Tara standing there, he got into the cab and gave the driver the Mulberry Street address.

As they turned to follow the trickle of cars and taxis, their dipped headlights like searching antennae, Bethany caught a glimpse of the other woman standing there dejectedly and felt sorry for her.

In a moment or two they had left the forecourt and joined the traffic still flowing through the streets of a city that never slept.

As they started to make their way downtown, Bethany tried to sort out her jumbled thoughts and feelings. Two things were uppermost in her mind. It was *Michael* that Tara had slept with, and when the girl had accused Joel of marrying *her* to punish them both he hadn't denied it.

His eyes on her face, Joel ordered quietly, 'Go on, spit it out.'

She took a deep breath. 'Why are you marrying me?'

'You've already asked me that question.'

'I asked you, but you didn't really give me an answer.'

Categorically, he said, 'I'm not marrying you to get my own back on Tara and Michael, if that's what you're thinking.'

'Oh…' She experienced such a rush of relief that momentarily she felt dizzy.

'I hope you believe me?'

'Yes, I do.' There had been a ring of truth in his voice that had left her in no doubt.

'Good.' He drew her to him and gave her a squeeze. 'I should hate it if Tara's venom poisoned your mind.'

The snow was coming faster now, small, feathery flakes that swirled and danced as they drifted down, gold and silver, caught in the headlights of the oncoming cars.

Sighing, she remarked, 'I love snow.'

'Though common sense insists that in town it's just a nuisance, so do I,' Joel admitted.

There was silence for a minute or so, then, harking back, he asked carefully, 'Apart from Tara, was the evening as bad as you'd feared?'

Bethany shook her head. 'No, everyone was very nice to me. Especially Lisa.'

'Lisa's a sweet kid. But not half as sweet as you.'

Warmed by his words, she nestled against him. It seemed he was starting to *like* her. Perhaps, given time, he might come to love her.

The future would have looked bright if only she had never met Michael… If only he hadn't wanted to marry her…

After a moment, with his usual acumen, Joel said, 'But there's still something bothering you?'

'It's Michael… I'm concerned about causing trouble between you,' she admitted.

His tone hard, uncompromising, Joel said, 'He'll be angry, I dare say. But he's unlikely to be heartbroken. And, knowing him, I'm pretty sure he'll soon bounce back.'

She bit her bottom lip and in a worried voice said, 'I just wish I'd told him straight away.'

'As it's much too late for regrets on that score, I suggest you stop worrying about it.' Gently, he added, 'Everything will work out fine, I'm sure.'

Cheered by his confidence, she made an effort to put the problem out of her mind.

After a while, finding the swish of the windscreen wipers soporific, she stifled a yawn.

'Tired?' Joel queried.

'A little.'

He drew her closer and, snuggled against him, she was almost asleep by the time they stopped outside the brownstone in Mulberry Street.

With an effort she roused herself and, climbing out, stood watching the softly falling snow caught in the golden halo of the street lamp like motes swimming in the beam of a spotlight.

It was a magical sight.

As soon as Joel had paid and tipped the driver, he turned to join her.

He was about to hurry her inside, when something about her stillness made him pause and look at her more closely. Then, as if under a spell, he remained stock still gazing down at her.

Her eyes were wide, her lips slightly parted and, framed by the soft, pale fur of her wrap, her lovely face looked luminous. Snowflakes spangled her dark hair and, as he watched, entranced, a couple settled on her long lashes, making her blink.

He hadn't intended to make love to her tonight, hadn't meant to touch her, but now he sighed softly and, as if there was no help for it, bent his head to kiss her.

Taken by surprise, it was a second before she responded, then she went into his arms gladly.

At first his lips felt cold, then he deepened the kiss and warmth spread through her until she glowed from head to toe.

Standing there in the falling snow, with Joel's arms wrapped around her and his mouth claiming hers, the rest of the world ceased to exist.

When, finally, he lifted his head and his voice husky, said, 'Let's get you indoors before you freeze,' in a kind of daze she allowed herself to be shepherded inside and up the stairs.

Once in their room, Joel lifted her wrap from her shoulders, gave it a shake and draped it over a chair. Then, when she straightened after removing her evening sandals, he produced a small towel he'd brought from the bathroom and handed it to her.

While she patted her hair dry he took off his jacket and tie, his movements measured and precise, and as she unfastened her earrings and put them on the dressing table he came round behind her and, bending his head, dropped a kiss on her nape.

Feeling the little shiver of pleasure that ran through her, he turned her into his arms and lifted her chin.

Looking up into his silvery eyes she saw they were dark and smoky with desire.

'You said earlier you were tired?'

Her heart picking up speed and new heat starting to spread through her, she answered, 'I am, a little.'

'But not too tired, I hope?'

'No,' she breathed, and reached up to wipe away a snowflake that had melted on his blond hair and was trickling down his cheek.

He turned his head to kiss her slim fingers before his mouth found hers. This time it was a light, controlled kiss that coaxed and teased and, for the moment at least, kept passion at bay.

Then his face intent, full of purpose, he began to undress her. Before the last wisp of underwear had been disposed of, a pool of liquid heat had formed in the pit of her stomach and she was quivering with desire and anticipation.

But, when she was naked, instead of stripping off his own clothes, he just discarded his shoes and socks and waited.

As she stood looking at him, his smile slightly mocking, he said, 'Fair's fair. Now you undress me.'

Though her fingers fumbled a little at their unaccustomed task, she undid the buttons of his silk shirt and, when he gave her no help, reached up to slip it off.

His chest and shoulders were broad and smoothly muscled with clear, healthy skin. Over his breastbone was a light scattering of golden hair which tapered to a vee and disappeared into the waistband of his trousers.

He looked eminently touchable and, longing to do just that, she reached out a cautious hand.

'Go ahead,' he invited. 'Touch me. I don't bite.'

Stroking her fingertips through the fine mat of curly hair, and fascinated by its silkiness, she leaned forward to rub her cheek against it.

Standing perfectly still, he made a low sound in his throat, as though urging her on.

Giving full rein to her impulse to touch and taste and know him, she turned her head and brushed her lips across his smoothly muscled expanse of chest until they reached a small, firm nipple. Then, her eyes closed and using the tip of her tongue, she explored its shape and size, its slightly rough, leathery texture.

His skin, fresh and clean and still carrying the faint scent of his shower gel, tasted slightly salty and, enjoying the novel sensation, she sucked and tugged a little, before biting delicately.

Feeling the tremor that ran through him, she felt a sense of power that she could give him at least some of the pleasure he had given her.

While her tongue and lips travelled on, learning the masculine secrets of flesh and muscle and bone, her hands slid down to the waistband of his trousers.

Bolder now, her fingers found and released the clip before sliding down the zip and easing the fine material over his lean hips. After a moment, his dark silk boxer shorts followed.

Stepping out of them, he pushed both garments aside with his foot and stood before her totally naked.

For a moment she simply stared at him, fascinated by his beauty, his sheer maleness.

'Go on,' he urged softly. 'Touch me; you know you want to.'

Reminding herself that this wasn't just a sexual encounter, that tomorrow he would be her husband, she let her hand follow the vee of hair downward, and heard the breath hiss through his teeth as her fingers found and caressed his firm flesh.

She was both excited and pleased by the knowledge that for the first time in her life she was making the running, making him feel the male equivalent of all the things he had made her feel.

Her triumph was short-lived.

With an inarticulate murmur, he caught her wrist and held her hand away from him. 'As things are, my love, your touch, though inexperienced, is too potent. It might be wise to take things more slowly.'

Conscious only that he'd called her *my love,* she made no protest when he lifted her on to the bed and proceeded to demonstrate precisely what he meant by slowly.

It wasn't until he'd almost driven her out of her mind that he answered her pleas and proceeded to give her the satisfaction she craved, before taking his own.

When she surfaced next morning she was alone in the big bed. Half asleep and half awake, she glanced blearily at her watch to find it was going up the hill for twelve o'clock.

Jolted into wakefulness by the realization that she was due to be married in a little over two hours, she sat bolt upright just as there was a tap at the door. Pulling up the duvet, she called, 'Come in.'

Molly appeared with a tray of coffee and scrambled eggs. 'Mr McAlister said if you weren't moving by eleven-thirty I was to bring this up.'

'Thank you,' Bethany said confusedly. 'I'm sorry to have given you all this trouble.'

'Why, bless you, it's no trouble. I've had all morning. I told Mr McAlister I would have plenty of time to do a small wedding buffet, but he said not to worry, all the arrangements are made and he's hired a firm of caterers.'

A note of excitement creeping into her voice, she went on, 'He asked Tom and me to come to the wedding and act as witnesses... That is if you haven't any objections?'

'Of course I haven't,' Bethany answered without hesitation. 'It'll be nice to have someone we know rather than a couple of strangers.'

Mrs Brannigan beamed.

Setting the tray carefully across Bethany's knees, she crossed the room to open the curtains, remarking as she did, 'I'm pleased to say it's a beautiful day. There's a light covering of fresh snow, but the sky's blue and the sun's shining. It's just perfect for a winter wedding.

'The flowers have arrived, so when you've had a bite to eat and showered I'll get Tom to bring them up along with the boxes and packages Dellon's delivered earlier.'

Then, in a burst of confidence, 'If I may say so, I'm pleased Mr McAlister's marrying a nice young lady like you. He's a fine man who deserves a good wife.'

'Have you been with him long?' Bethany asked, between sips of coffee.

'I was his mother's housekeeper until she died and I've been with him since. In all those months I've never known him to raise his voice or get in a temper, even though at times young Mr Michael must have tried his patience sorely—'

Molly pulled herself up short and, obviously afraid she'd let her tongue run away with her, murmured hurriedly, 'Well, I'd better be getting along.'

At the door she paused to say, 'I understand that Miss Harvey's going to be your bridesmaid, but if you need any help before the young lady gets here, just let me know.'

'Thanks, I will.'

Though she was too excited to be hungry, Bethany ate the scrambled eggs, which were light and fluffy, before going to clean her teeth and shower.

When she returned to the bedroom wrapped in a towelling robe, her hair still slightly damp, a pile of black and gold packages and a florist's cellophane box were waiting.

The box contained a bridal bouquet of pale yellow rosebuds and fragrant stephanotis and a matching bridesmaid's posy.

She had just finished admiring them when there was a tap at the door and a voice called, 'Hi, it's me.'

Bethany opened the door to find Lisa, slightly dishevelled and flushed with excitement, hovering outside clutching a handbag and several of the now familiar black and gold boxes.

Catching the top one, which had started to slip, Bethany invited, 'Come on in. Did you manage to get all you needed?'

Dropping her bag and packages on the nearest chair, Lisa said happily, 'Oh, yes. Joel drove me to Dellon's and they took care of everything.'

'That's great.'

All at once, wanting very much to see Joel, needing the reassurance of his presence, Bethany asked, 'Did he come back with you?'

'Yes, he's downstairs. He said to tell you he'll see you in church.'

'Oh…' A little deflated, Bethany wondered if he was merely busy or following the tradition of the groom not seeing the bride prior to the wedding.

Lisa sighed. 'Isn't it romantic being swept off your feet like that? You must feel so excited.'

'I feel rather like Alice in Wonderland. Nothing's quite real—' Breaking off, Bethany added with a shaky smile, 'I'll be a married woman in less than two hours and I still haven't told my parents. I intended to ring them first thing this morning, but I'm afraid I overslept.'

Seeing the shadow that fell across her face, Lisa suggested practically, 'Well, I know there isn't much time, but if I get on and unpack everything, couldn't you tell them now?'

While the younger girl emptied the boxes and laid everything out neatly on the bed, Bethany tapped in the international code and the familiar Notting Hill number of her parents' home.

It rang three or four times, then she heard the click as the receiver was lifted.

'Hello?' It was her father's voice.

'Dad, it's me…'

'Well, hello, love.'

'I've some news for you and Mum…'

'You can tell me, but I'm afraid your mother's not here. She's staying at her sister's for a few days.'

With a guilty feeling of relief—her mother was an inveterate talker—Bethany quickly and concisely told her father the bare facts.

He listened without interrupting.

When she finished he said seriously, 'It all seems very sudden, but you've always been a sensible girl, so I presume you know what you're doing… I take it you love him?'

'Yes, I love him,' she said steadily.

'Then you have my blessing. When you get back, I'd like to meet my new son-in-law.'

'Of course. I think you'll like him. Will you explain to Mum, and tell her I'm sorry to spring it on you both like this?'

'I'll do that. All our love…'

Bethany replaced the receiver, then, obeying an impulse, picked it up again and tapped in Michael's number. If she could just talk to him briefly and tell him she was sorry, it would take a weight off her mind.

But he didn't seem to be answering and she gave it up for the time being.

Lisa glanced across to smile at her. 'What a beautiful wedding dress… And Joel was quite right, the bridesmaid's dress will go perfectly.

'By the way, he said the cars will be arriving about one-thirty, so we haven't a lot of time.'

'Oh, Lord,' Bethany muttered, 'and I've still got to pack some things to take away.'

'If you find a case and get out everything you need I'll pack while you do your hair and make-up.'

'Thanks,' Bethany said gratefully, producing a case and starting to pile stuff on a chair. 'I don't know what I would have done without you.'

Looking pleased, Lisa began to pack swiftly and efficiently, while Bethany made-up lightly and brushed and coiled her hair.

'Where are you going on honeymoon?' Lisa asked as, her packing finished, she helped Bethany into her dress. 'Or is it a secret?'

'We're having a few days in the Catskills. Joel's driving us up after the wedding.'

'Sounds great,' Lisa remarked enthusiastically.

Having fastened the tiny covered buttons that ran down the back of the dress, she said, 'It fits like a dream…' Then, hastily, 'Oh, I mustn't forget…'

From her bag she took a small blue velvet case. 'Joel asked me to say he'd like you to wear these. They belonged to his grandmother.'

The case contained a double string of perfectly graded lustrous pearls and a pair of beautiful pearl-drop earrings.

'He said he meant to give them to you last night, but somehow he got distracted.'

When, blushing and misty-eyed, Bethany had donned the necklace and earrings, Lisa set her coronet in place and arranged the short filmy veil.

Stepping back to admire her handiwork, she exclaimed, 'Wow! You look sensational. Joel will be bowled over.'

While Bethany slipped into her shoes and took the flowers out of their cellophane wrapping, Lisa quickly did her own hair and face and put on her pretty apricot silk bridesmaid's dress, a matching headband and a silver necklace.

'What a pretty necklace,' Bethany remarked.

Lisa looked delighted. 'Yes, isn't it? Joel insisted on buying it for me as a bridesmaid's thank you present.'

Then, reaching for her bag, from a piece of tissue paper she produced a dainty garter embroidered with blue butterflies and asked, a shade diffidently, 'By the way, I wondered if you'd like to borrow this?

'You know the old wedding rhyme,' she went on. "Something old, something new, something borrowed and something blue"…? Well, you have something old and something new and I thought…' Looking a little flustered, she broke off.

Swallowing the lump in her throat, Bethany said warmly, 'What a lovely idea. I'd be delighted to borrow it.' Lifting her silken skirts, she slipped the garter on and settled it above her right knee.

There was a tap at the door and Molly, attired in her best hat, a flower pinned to her jacket, appeared to announce that the caterers were here and both the bridesmaid's car and the bridal car were waiting.

Picking up her posy, Lisa said, 'I should go first, shouldn't I?' Then, suddenly nervous, needing reassurance, 'Will I do?'

'You look lovely,' Bethany said sincerely.

Lisa beamed. 'It *is* a pretty dress, isn't it? David's picking me up after the wedding. I hope he gets here in time to see it.'

As the younger girl, flushed with pride and excitement, hurried away, Molly added cheerfully, 'And Senator Harvey's just arrived. He's waiting in the hall.'

'Perhaps you'll tell him I'll be down in just a minute? Then, if you and Tom want to get off…'

When Molly had gone, Bethany swapped her engagement ring to her right hand, gathered up her bouquet and took a last look in the mirror before making her way down the stairs.

Having stood and watched her descend, the Senator, smartly dressed in a grey pinstripe suit and with a cream carnation in his buttonhole, said, 'My dear, you look absolutely radiant.'

'Thank you.' She smiled at him. 'I must say you look very smart yourself.'

He preened a little before asking, 'All ready?'

'All ready.'

'Then we mustn't keep the groom waiting.' He offered her his arm.

It was another clear, cold day with sunshine gilding the skeletal trees and ricocheting from the windscreens of passing cars as they drove to the Church of the Holy Shepherd.

The lovely old building, with its elegant spires and intricate stonework, was sandwiched between two skyscrapers. It should have looked incongruous, but somehow it didn't. Its air of timeless beauty, of *belonging*, contrived to make its glass and concrete neighbours look like modern upstarts.

As the Senator helped Bethany from the car, a photographer appeared and began to take pictures, backing into the church in front of them.

Inside it was serene and dim, despite the bright shafts of light slanting through the stained glass windows and the lighted candles. The scent of flowers hung on the still air and in the background an organ was playing softly.

Joel, wearing a well-cut grey suit, a cream carnation in his buttonhole and looking like every woman's dream of a handsome bridegroom, was waiting by the chancel steps, Paul Rosco beside him.

Apart from Molly and Tom, the rows of polished pews were empty.

Lisa was standing at the back of the church with the Reverend

John Daintree who, after greeting them, went to take his place in front of the altar.

The organist changed to Bach and, as Bethany walked up the aisle on the Senator's arm, Joel turned to smile at her.

Since leaving Mulberry Street nothing had seemed quite real and, feeling as though she was dreaming the whole thing, she handed her bouquet to Lisa and moved to stand by her bridegroom's side.

When, after a second or two, the organ music faded into silence, the Reverend John Daintree cleared his throat and began the service. 'Dearly beloved…'

Afterwards, though the dreamlike state still persisted, Bethany retained a clear, jewel-bright memory of the ceremony. The firmness of Joel's responses; his serious expression as he slipped the gold wedding band on to her finger; the joy as they were pronounced man and wife; the feeling of coming home as he turned back her veil and kissed her.

But her most treasured memory was her surprise when the best man produced not one ring but two and her gladness as she slid the heavy gold signet ring on to Joel's finger.

When the wedding certificate had been signed and witnessed, there were handshakes and kisses all round. Then more photographs were taken before the Senator left for La Guardia, Paul returned to his office and the Reverend John Daintree began to get ready for his next engagement.

Once outside, the bride and groom were showered with rice before they and the remainder of the wedding party returned in convoy to Mulberry Street.

When they arrived they found a young man with fair curly hair and a thin intelligent face waiting on the front stairs. 'Sorry, I'm afraid I'm early,' David remarked apologetically when Lisa had introduced them. 'I'll take a walk and come back in half an hour or so.'

'You'll do no such thing,' Joel said firmly. 'We need you to even up the numbers.'

'Please do come in and have something to eat and a glass of champagne,' Bethany added persuasively.

'Well, if you're sure?'

She smiled at him. 'Quite sure.'

As he escorted Lisa up the steps, Bethany heard him say, 'You look beautiful,' and was pleased to note that the younger girl went pink with pleasure.

In the event she wasn't the only one. As they reached the door, Bethany was swept, blushing and laughing, into Joel's arms and carried over the threshold.

'I believe in keeping up old traditions,' he told a grinning David.

'I must say I approve,' that young man said. 'So long as the bride is as slim as Bethany and Lisa,' he said with a grin.

In the dining room the caterers had set out a small but excellent buffet with fresh flowers, a beautifully decorated wedding cake and some perfectly chilled champagne.

Joel insisted that Molly and Tom joined them, which they did as soon as Tom had brought the car round to the door and loaded the luggage into the boot.

After the party of six had done justice to the meal, Bethany, Joel's arm round her waist, his hand over hers, cut the cake.

Then, when their glasses had been refilled, David, standing in for the best man, proved to be unexpectedly eloquent as he proposed a toast to the bride and groom.

The toast over, he announced that Lisa and he ought to be moving, while Molly and Tom, who both declared they were woozy, slipped off quietly.

Because he was driving later Joel had drunk very little, but after two glasses of the vintage champagne Bethany too had started to feel pleasantly floaty and light-headed.

Having given the caterers permission to clear away, Joel took David through to the living room, where he looked at the evening paper while the other three went upstairs to change.

When the two girls returned carrying their outdoor things, they saw that Joel, who had used the spare room to change into smart casuals, was in his study apparently reading his emails.

Seeing them pass his partly open door, he abandoned what he was doing and returned to the living-room to see Lisa and David off.

'If it's okay with you,' Lisa said, as the two men shook hands and the women exchanged warm hugs, 'I'll call and collect the rest of my things when you get back from your honeymoon.'

'Of course,' Bethany told her.

'And you must see the photographs,' Joel said. He added, 'Then perhaps we could make up a foursome for dinner and dancing?'

Looking as if she'd been given a present, Lisa cried, 'Oh, that would be great,' and got David's nod of approval.

When the pair had been waved off, Joel, appearing happy and relaxed, as though any underlying tension with regard to the wedding had drained away, gathered Bethany close. 'Alone at last,' he said deeply. 'Do you realize, woman, that you've been my wife for almost two hours and I still haven't kissed you properly?'

Lifting her face to his, she suggested, 'I'm sure you could remedy that.'

'I fully intend to. In fact, had we changed together, I would have done rather more than simply kiss you. But, unfortunately, the presence of a bridesmaid, no matter how sweet, is inhibiting.'

Looking at him from beneath long lashes, she asked, 'How soon do we have to start?'

'We can start whenever we want to.'

'In that case,' she began demurely, 'as Lisa's no longer here…'

He laughed and, his silvery-green eyes gleaming, said, 'What a s-sensible woman you are.'

She pretended to be disappointed. 'I thought you were going to say sexy.'

'Oh, you're that too.' Then, punctuating the words with soft baby kisses, 'Not to mention sensuous and seductive and sensational… Can you think of any other suitable words beginning with an s…?'

Enjoying this lighter side he was showing, she suggested, 'Spellbinding…'

'Undoubtedly the best yet.' With a little growl, he swept her up in his arms. 'Come on then, my little witch, let's go somewhere more private and make mad, passionate love…'

Gladness and joy bubbling inside her, and knowing she'd never been so happy in her life, she put her arms round his neck and gave herself up to the promise of delight.

They were halfway to the door when it was thrown open abruptly and Michael, looking flushed and dishevelled, burst into the room.

Joel froze and after a second or two put Bethany down and steadied her until she had found her balance. Then, looking at the newcomer, his face set and grim, he asked quietly, 'What the devil are you doing here?'

CHAPTER TEN

IGNORING his stepmother and looking at Bethany, Michael said hoarsely, 'Tara seemed to think you and Joel were planning to get married, and I came to warn you not to be taken in by—'

Catching sight of her left hand where her new wedding ring gleamed, he broke off and muttered an angry oath. Then, after a moment, 'But it seems I'm too late. Who said money talks?'

'I didn't marry Joel for his money.'

'Well, as you've only known him five minutes, it must have been love at first sight,' he sneered.

Bethany raised her chin in a gesture of defiance. 'As a matter of fact, it was.'

For a moment he stared at her, then he said bitterly, 'Do you know, I'm almost inclined to believe you. You said you couldn't marry me because you didn't love me, now you look like a woman in love, the epitome of a happy bride—'

'Michael, I'm sorry,' Bethany broke in. 'I should have told you straight away how things were. I know I've treated you badly and I—'

Brushing her apology aside, he went on, 'But you won't look quite so happy when I tell you exactly why the swine married you.'

Lifting her chin, she said, 'I already know about Tara and you, and I don't believe—'

'Tara has nothing to do with this. What has *everything* to do with it is that when I marry I become independent. My own master. As soon as probate is granted I can sell the blasted house and raise some cash.'

'But I thought—'

'The terms of Grandmother's will state that I can sell the house either when I'm twenty-five or when I "settle down and marry". Big brother didn't want that. It takes away his power. He was determined to stop you marrying me...'

There was some truth in that last statement, as Bethany well knew. She could still hear the ring of steel in Joel's voice as he'd told her, "Well, get this into your pretty little head, there's no way I'll allow you to marry him".

When she had asked him why, he'd answered, "Perhaps I'm jealous. Perhaps I want you for myself".

She had wanted desperately to believe that, and had *almost* succeeded in doing so. But maybe she had been wrong? Maybe he had had other reasons?

'And the only way he could be *sure* you wouldn't,' Michael went on, 'was to marry you himself.'

After a moment's thought, she said firmly, 'That's utter rubbish. I'd already told him I had no intention of marrying you.'

Michael smirked. 'It seems he didn't believe you.'

'Even if he didn't, no man in his right senses would tie himself to a woman he didn't want just to stop her marrying his stepbrother.

'In any case, if you were set on getting married, how could he stop you?'

'He bought Glenda off,' Michael said resentfully.

'If she was willing to be bought off, she couldn't have loved you,' Bethany pointed out quietly. 'And there must be plenty of nice women who would jump at the chance to marry you.'

Michael laughed at her innocence. 'Sam, the girl I'm bunking down with, would marry me like a shot if I asked her, but—'

He stopped short, looking a bit sheepish. Then, with a shrug, muttered, 'Oh, what the hell! I know I told you I was flatsharing with a friend, but when you wouldn't come across... Well, a man has needs and—'

'It really doesn't matter,' Bethany said. She added crisply, 'So why don't you go ahead and ask her?'

He sighed. 'I considered that a few months ago, but I realized she was a mercenary bitch who would take me for everything I had if we split up.

'Then, after I met you, no one else would do. *You* were the one I wanted. As soon as Big Brother realized that, he stepped in...'

As Bethany began to shake her head, Michael went on angrily, 'He's prepared to go to any lengths to keep control of my life, even to marrying a woman he believes is a liar and a thief—'

'That's quite enough.' Joel's words were softly spoken but they fell like a whiplash.

Though he looked scared, Michael faced up to his stepbrother. '*I* know you're wrong about that, but don't try to tell me it isn't what *you* believe. I *know* what you were out to prove, about the trap you set for her. That loopy old woman let the cat out of the bag.' Michael carried on regardless of the warning look in his stepbrother's eyes.

'I happened to be at your flat picking up some of my clothes when she phoned. She thought she was talking to you. You'll no doubt be surprised to know that she's "found" the things she assured you had been stolen—'

He stopped speaking abruptly and backed away as Joel took a step towards him.

'Don't worry,' Joel said grimly. 'I've no intention of laying a finger on you. However, it's high time you stopped and listened to some straight speaking.

'You're blaming me for trying to control your life but all I've done is try to protect you, to keep you out of trouble, as I promised our Grandmother.'

'Damn it all, I don't want your help…' Michael began to bluster.

'You may not want it, but you certainly *need* it. You're nothing but a young fool who, at the rate you're going, will end up penniless and in real trouble…'

Upset and agitated, needing a chance to think, Bethany turned on her heel and fled into Joel's study.

Her legs feeling oddly shaky, barely able to support her, she sank down on the black leather swivel chair by his desk.

Michael's words, 'He's prepared to go to any lengths to keep control of my life, even to marrying a woman he believes is a liar and a thief…' seemed branded on her mind.

And Joel had said, 'All I've done is try to protect you, to keep you out of trouble…' Which was virtually admitting it.

The feeling of warmth and trust that exchanging rings had brought shrivelled and died and a kind of bewildered anger took its place.

Joel might believe she'd lied, but what possible justification had he for believing she was a thief?

What was it Michael had said? 'I know what you were out to prove, about the trap you set for her. That loopy old woman let the cat out of the bag…'

But that didn't make any sense… Unless…

Recalling the evening she and Joel had met, the night they had spent together at Dunscar, his questions, his marked interest in her job, light began to dawn.

'The loopy old woman' had to be Mrs Deramack, and the 'trap' he had set must have been connected to her visit to Bosthwaite to look at the antiques.

He must have planted something there, something small and

valuable, that a dishonest person, thinking they were dealing with a confused old woman, could easily have slipped into a pocket or a handbag.

But to have set up a trap of any kind he must have known about her visit in advance.

Which raised the question—how much else had he known about her? Obviously about her job and presumably about her relationship—innocent as it was—with Michael.

So did that mean he knew Michael had been selling things to Feldon Antiques?

If he did that would account for his interest in the bracelet she had been wearing. He'd obviously recognized it as belonging to his mother's set.

Guessing she'd bought it from Michael and believing that the stones were rubies, had he assumed that she'd cheated his step-brother and paid a lot less for it than it was worth?

Or—her stomach tightened as an even worse thought struck her—had he suspected her of stealing it?

If he had, and he'd known of—or possibly even *arranged?*— her visit to the Lake District to see Mrs Deramack, their meeting that night hadn't been a chance one.

Or perhaps in a way it had?

Maybe he hadn't actually *intended* them to meet. Maybe he had simply been tailing her that day. She recalled how a similar Range Rover to the one he'd been driving had followed her on her outward journey. If it hadn't been for the flat tyre and the fog, he might have just followed her back to the Dundale Inn. But, as circumstances had thrown them together and altered his plans, he had turned the meeting to his advantage. Had used the opportunity to check her out and try to confirm her guilt.

A hollow feeling in the pit of her stomach, she recalled the jammed zip in her handbag and the way her phone had been replaced in the wrong pocket.

He must have searched through her bag in the belief that his plan had worked, that she'd stolen whatever it was he'd planted, because Mrs Deramack had told him so.

'You'll no doubt be surprised to know that she's "found" the things she assured you had been stolen…'

Bethany bit her lip. Still at least he now knew she was innocent on that score. But what if Michael hadn't admitted selling the vase and other things to Feldon Antiques? What if Joel thought *she* had contrived to steal them?

Oh, surely not?

Yet it made a terrible kind of sense.

Suppose he'd believed her to be an unscrupulous liar and a thief and had been afraid she might marry a besotted Michael and take him for everything he had, what would have been the best way to deal with it?

One sure way to protect his stepbrother would be to marry her himself.

But, being no fool, he had first taken steps to protect himself. That was why he had insisted on a marriage contract.

For the first time she realized the full significance of the phone call she had overheard and, with excellent verbal recall, played it through in her mind.

'It's of the utmost importance…' Joel had said. 'I need the document ready to be signed by tomorrow afternoon…'

Then, 'Yes… Yes… Exactly as I've outlined…'

Paul Rosco must have said something like, *But will she forget your stepbrother and marry you?*

And Joel had responded, 'Well, at the moment, as far as money and power goes, I'm the best bet. And, however you look at it, the organ grinder has got to be a better proposition than the monkey…

'Yes, Paul, I know it must seem drastic to you, and I admit it's taking a big risk, but I can't see any other way. And I assure you that whether it works or not it has its compensations...

'Yes, yes... If there's any way I can *make* it work, I'm prepared to stick with it...'

And what would Paul Rosco have said? Something like, *But suppose she tries to take you for a ride?*

And Joel had answered, 'I can't rule it out. That's why I want to be sure I can't be ripped off...'

For the first time she understood why the solicitor had been so cool and guarded with her. He had known why Joel was marrying her in such haste and, regarding her as a scheming little bitch, disapproved of the whole thing...

Trying to blink back tears of anger and humiliation, Bethany bent her head, feeling wretched, sick and hollow inside.

At that instant the door opened and Joel strode in. With a glance at her stricken face, he said, 'I'm sorry you had to find out like this.'

As she opened her mouth to speak, he added, 'I can see how upset you are, but we'll have plenty of time to clear the air when we get to the cabin.' Briskly, he added, 'There's snow forecast for later tonight, so it's time we got going...'

She fought the urge to laugh hysterically. Did he seriously think she was going to meekly go on honeymoon with him as if nothing was wrong?

But instinctively she knew that he would brook no alteration to his plans and it would be difficult, not to say impossible, to fight him.

But somehow she *had* to get away.

Gathering up the papers from his desk, he put them in his briefcase and said, 'Michael's staying here tonight, so while you collect your coat and bag I'll just have a quick word with Molly.'

Bethany felt her heart leap. It was the chance she needed.

To run in that way would mean leaving all her belongings and she had no dollars, but she could give the driver English money and use her credit card to get a flight back to London.

To her great relief there was no sign of Michael and as soon as Joel had gone in search of the housekeeper she hastily pulled on her coat and gathered up her shoulder bag.

A moment later she had let herself out of the front door and was hurrying down the steps. Joel's sleek saloon was standing by the kerb and she wished fleetingly that she had the keys.

There were no taxis in sight and, her coat flapping open, she set off down the lamplit street at a trot. She had almost reached the end when she heard her name called and, glancing back, saw Joel in pursuit.

Running now, she turned the corner and started along Mulberry Square. She had only gone a short distance when she saw a yellow cab coming towards her and waved frantically.

The driver did a U-turn and a few seconds later he was drawing up beside her. Pulling open the door, she scrambled in and said breathlessly, 'JFK please, as fast as you can.'

Sinking back in her seat, she fastened her safety belt and sighed with relief.

They had left Mulberry Square behind them and were halfway along Brand Street when they were held up by a red light.

Suddenly the door was yanked open, her seat belt was unfastened and a moment later she was half hauled, half lifted, out on to the sidewalk.

'Leave me alone. Let me go…' She struggled to free herself.

The cab driver turned to see what was happening and, lowering his window began, 'Hey there, what's going on?'

As passers-by looked in their direction, Joel pulled her into his arms and kissed her, stifling her attempts to protest.

Then, holding her firmly with one arm, he thrust a handful of dollar bills at the driver and said, 'Sorry about this. We've only been married a few hours and this is our first quarrel—'

Making a fresh attempt to pull free, Bethany cried, 'This wasn't just a quarrel and you know it. Now let me go, I'm leaving…'

In a long-suffering voice, Joel said, 'Women do make mountains out of molehills…'

'Don't I know it! Well, best of luck, pal!'

'Please, driver, don't listen to him. I want to—' But Bethany's plea fell on deaf ears as the lights changed and the cab moved forward.

Despite her protests she was hustled to where Joel's car, its door still standing open, was holding up the stream of evening traffic.

Fairly bundling her inside, he clicked the seat belt into place and slammed the door.

As he went round to the driver's side, she fumbled for the door handle, but the door wouldn't open. Gritting her teeth, she realized he must have put some kind of child-lock into place.

A moment later they were underway, the traffic began to flow again and the little incident was over and done with.

Taking a deep breath, she said as steadily as possible, 'If you think you can make me go on honeymoon with you as if nothing has happened, you're quite wrong. I'm leaving you.'

'Perhaps when we've had a chance to talk you'll change your mind.'

'There's nothing you could say or do that will make me change my mind, so if you'll please stop the car and let me get out, I'll take a taxi to the airport.'

He showed no sign of obeying and, glancing at his handsome profile, noting the set of his jaw, she knew she was wasting her breath.

Having achieved what he'd set out to achieve, and thinking so badly of her, why couldn't he just let her go? she wondered bleakly. But, even as her mind formed the question, she knew the answer.

No doubt against his will, and in spite of his better judgement, he still wanted her physically.

Well, he might still want her, but no matter how much she loved him, her pride wouldn't let her go on with this mockery of a honeymoon.

Knowing, however, that further protests would be of no avail, she sat in resentful silence while they made their way out of the city.

True to the forecast, it had started to snow and, despite the traffic, the road was soon covered, the tracks of the cars ahead making continuous black patterns against the white.

For a while Bethany watched the swirling flakes before, physically weary and emotionally exhausted, she drifted into sleep.

Fingers stroking her cheek awakened her. Lifting her head, she opened heavy eyes to find they had stopped in a small snowy clearing surrounded by trees.

In front of them was a one-storey clapboard house with a wooden veranda running round it. The long square-paned windows were lit and a lantern in the open porch spilled a pool of yellow light.

Still half asleep, she stumbled a little as Joel helped her out and he put an arm around her as they climbed the wooden steps and crossed the porch to the white-painted door.

It was unlocked and the trail of fresh footprints in the snow between the car and the house showed that he had taken their luggage inside before waking her.

The big living room, with its rustic furniture, was warm and welcoming, though the fire in the stove had died to a red glow.

His arm still encircling her, he asked, 'Would you like anything to eat or drink?'

Longing only to drift back into sleep, she shook her head.

'Then straight to bed, I think.'

'I won't sleep with you.'

Silkily, he asked, 'Have you considered that you may have no choice in the matter? You're my wife.'

Pushing his arm away, she said, 'I'm not your *wife* and I've no intention of ever being your wife. Knowing what you think of me—'

'But you *don't* know what I think of you.'

Swaying a little, she insisted thickly, 'I don't want to sleep with you, and if you force me to I'll never forgive you.'

He sighed. 'Very well. Until things are sorted out, I'll use the other room.'

The bedroom he led her to was as warm and comfortable as the living room had been and the double bed looked soft and cosy.

Her small case had been placed on a blanket chest and, like a zombie, neither thinking nor feeling, she found her toilet things and cleaned her teeth in the *en-suite* bathroom.

She returned to the bedroom to find her nightdress and dressing-gown had been laid out on the bed and the duvet turned back.

There was no sign of Joel.

When she had taken off her clothes and donned her nightie she climbed into bed, turned out the light and slept as soon as her head touched the pillow.

She awoke to the appetizing aroma of freshly brewed coffee and bacon frying. Climbing out of bed, she drew aside the heavy folkweave curtains and looked through the window at a winter wonderland.

Hemlock and pine, their green arms weighed down with snow,

stood at the edge of the clearing. On the opposite slopes she could see a scattering of houses and, in the far distance, snow-covered mountains.

It was a beautiful, secluded place, perfect for a romantic honeymoon, if only things had been other than they were.

But after almost believing that her dreams had come true and she had everything she had ever wanted in life—even a chance to win Joel's love—she had ended up with nothing.

Less than nothing, as he thought so badly of her.

Feeling empty and desolate, she went through to the bathroom to clean her teeth and shower, before dressing in fine wool trousers and a cream sweater.

Though she dreaded the thought of having to confront him, the sooner she could convince him that she had no intention of going through with this marriage, the better. Then, hopefully, he would take her back to New York City.

As she brushed her hair she glanced in the mirror. A vulnerable-looking woman with bleak, disillusioned, cloudy-grey eyes, too big for her pale face, stared back at her.

She turned away abruptly and, leaving her long dark hair loose about her shoulders, her head held high, made her way to the kitchen to face Joel.

The sophisticated city man who owned a jet plane, wore silk shirts and hand-tailored suits, was gone. Dressed in jeans and a dark blue shirt open at the throat, he was standing by the stove, turning sizzling bacon in a pan.

'Excellent timing,' he greeted her cheerfully. 'I'm just about ready to dish up.'

'I'm not hungry. I need to talk to you.'

He looked at her squarely. 'We'll talk as soon as we've eaten.'

A glance at his face told her she would get nowhere unless she did things his way, so she allowed herself to be seated at the table.

The big kitchen was warm and homely, with a black wood-stove and natural pine furniture. On the table was a pitcher of freshly squeezed orange juice and two glasses, a crusty sourdough loaf, butter, blueberry jam and a jug of cream.

He helped her to orange juice before filling two plates with crispy bacon and fluffy scrambled eggs. Then, sitting down opposite, he waited for her to begin her breakfast.

Feeling anything but hungry, she picked up her knife and fork.

After a moment he followed suit and, his eyes on her face, observed, 'With your hair loose like that and no make-up you look about seventeen.'

She made no comment and he relapsed into silence.

When their plates were empty and the coffee was finished, he led the way over to where two cushioned chairs were drawn up in front of the glowing stove.

As soon as they were both seated he began without preamble. 'Some months ago I discovered that a very valuable antique bowl appeared to be missing from my grandmother's house. Michael, the only person apart from myself who had a key to Lanervic Square, denied all knowledge of it.

'When, over the next few weeks, other smaller items started to disappear at regular intervals, I hired a private detective.

'He found that Michael had a girlfriend who was a buyer for Feldon Antiques and—'

'And, suspecting me of stealing them, you arranged for me to visit Mrs Deramack and set a trap...'

A wry twist to his mouth, Joel admitted, 'Though I'm not proud of it, at the time it seemed the best way to obtain some proof. So I asked her to phone Feldon Antiques and say she had some pieces of silver and porcelain for sale.

'When I was sure you were going, I planted two valuable silver vinaigrettes amongst a jumble of worthless stuff in the parlour.

'I was keeping an eye on you and after you'd left I phoned Alice and she told me the vinaigrettes were missing. I believed her, having failed to realize just how senile the old lady has become—'

'Then you saw me wearing the bracelet and jumped to the conclusion that I'd stolen that too,' Bethany said bitterly.

He shook his head. 'The set had been in my mother's wall safe in what used to be her bedroom, but was now Michael's when he came over to New York. So he was the only person who could possibly have taken it.

'I presumed you'd bought it from him—'

'And you took it, believing I'd paid him for garnets when they were actually rubies—'

'I took it to a jeweller to get to the truth. When he confirmed that they were garnets I was delighted.'

She shook her head, denying his statement. 'You believed I was a thief and a liar—'

'I *suspected* you might be. And when I questioned you and you wouldn't tell me the truth…

'I realize now you were just trying to protect Michael, but then I—'

She cut him off. 'You thought I was an unscrupulous bitch who had battened on to him and, knowing you could deal with me better, you married me to protect him.'

'I kept trying to tell myself that was why I was doing it,' Joel admitted, 'but in the end I married you because I wanted you to be my wife—'

'I don't believe you,' she broke in furiously. 'I overheard your conversation with Paul Rosco. I know exactly what you thought of me, why you insisted on a marriage contract.

'Well, I've no intention of staying with you, but don't worry, the only thing I want from you is my freedom. I've still got a job so I'll be—'

'That's just it, you haven't.' He cut in authoritatively. 'I've already made it clear to your boss that you won't be going back.'

'How dare you?' she choked. 'You've no right to make decisions for me. Whether or not I go back to Feldon's is none of your business.'

His voice remained calm as he replied. 'You're my wife, which makes it my business. And there's no way I'll allow you to go back there.'

'If you think for one minute—' Bethany was furious.

'Stansfield, the detective I hired, found that the police are interested in Feldon. They suspect him of dealing in stolen property, and it should be only a matter of time before they catch him.'

Though she herself had had doubts about the scrupulousness of Tony's business methods, she had never thought that he might be seriously crooked.

'I don't believe it,' she said without conviction.

Joel passed her a couple of sheets of paper. 'After I'd got changed yesterday I checked my emails and found this waiting. I suggest you read it.'

The email read:

After further and more extensive enquiries, I can find no proof that Miss Seaton is anything other than honest. While she is still officially Feldon's buyer, since Tony Feldon took over the business on his father's death he has made himself responsible for all the pricing and buying.

His father, James Feldon, whom Miss Seaton worked for for almost four years, had an excellent reputation for fair and honest dealing.

However, it appears that his son is under police scrutiny. They suspect him of dealing in stolen property, which apparently he sells on to wealthy private collectors who don't ask questions.

With regard to the missing bowl, I've managed to take a look through the register that Feldon keeps. There is no record of any such bowl being either bought or sold.

That being the case, it will be extremely difficult, not to say impossible, to prove anything against Feldon, unless your stepbrother will admit to selling him the vase.

Following the line of enquiry you advised, I found that some three months ago your stepbrother paid over a very considerable sum in gambling debts. Which strongly indicates that he *did* sell the bowl. Though what he appears to have received for it suggests that it hadn't been properly identified as Ming…

Going cold, Bethany admitted, 'I saw the bowl…'

His silvery-green eyes narrowing, Joel asked, 'What did you think?'

Through stiff lips, she said, 'I thought it was Ming, but Tony said he'd taken it to an expert on Chinese porcelain who had identified it as Qing. Which, of course, made it worth a lot less.'

'I see,' Joel said quietly.

After a moment she returned her attention to the email, which continued:

Since then your stepbrother has run up new, and considerable, gambling debts. However, he has no more money left and he is using your name to obtain credit.

I don't hold out much hope of getting any further with my enquiries and, as you are adamant that you don't want to involve the police, I'll wait to hear from you…

As Bethany looked up, Joel said grimly, 'Feldon Antiques appears to have made a killing on the bowl but, of course, having stolen it himself, Michael wasn't in a position to argue.'

'Perhaps he shouldn't have sold it until after probate has been granted, but how can you call it *stealing* when it belonged to him?' she objected.

'It didn't belong to him,' Joel said flatly, 'nor did the other things he sold. The house itself is his, but the contents were bequeathed to my aunt and uncle who intend to auction them and retire on the proceeds.'

Stricken, she admitted, 'Tony wasn't interested in the smaller items. I bought those for my collection, along with the bracelet.'

'Well, don't worry about it. Even though, when I talked to Michael yesterday, he finally admitted taking the bowl and other things, I can't imagine they will want to press charges. Especially if I make up the shortfall.

'Which I've agreed to do, as well as pay off his current gambling debts, but only on condition that he takes the post I've offered him in Los Angeles, sorts out his gambling problem and keeps to the straight and narrow.'

There was silence for a little while, then Joel asked quietly, 'Do you feel any happier now you know the truth?'

Still icy cold and resentful inside, she demanded, 'Why should I feel any happier? The truth is, you married me believing me to be a thief and a liar. Married me to save Michael…'

He took her hand and looked into her eyes. 'The truth is I wanted you and was jealous of Michael from the word go. I shouldn't have seduced you that night, but I couldn't help myself.

'I tried to fight it, but after a couple of days of knowing you I no longer cared what you might or might not have done. I was so madly in love with you I would always have married you and done my best to make it work.' She tried to remain impassive to his dazzling smile but her heart leapt at his words.

Joel continued. 'If Michael hadn't burst in when he did I'd intended to tell you everything when we got back from honeymoon, and ask your forgiveness.' Joel reached up and tenderly stroked her face with the back of his hand. 'I just hope you can understand why I acted as I did. But I didn't know you then. Finding that you're blameless, as lovely and innocent inside as you are out, is the best gift I've ever received.'

His words and his obvious sincerity warmed her like a blazing fire on a bleak winter's day, thawing the ice and dissipating any lingering resentment.

'From the moment I set eyes on you, I was lost,' he went on quietly. 'In some strange way I felt as if you were already under my skin, in my heart, in my bloodstream. Part of me. I felt as if I'd known and loved you for years.

'When you said you wouldn't marry a man you didn't love, and then you told Michael it had been love at first sight, I began to hope that a miracle had happened and that you felt the same way about me...'

Bethany rose to her feet a shade unsteadily and saw the look of despair on his face when he thought she was leaving.

He caught her hand. 'Please don't go. I know you must feel angry and bitter but—'

She stooped and her kiss stopped his words.

With a sound almost like a groan, his arms went around her and he pulled her on to his knee.

It was a little while before they surfaced, then he said huskily, 'Tell me I'm not dreaming this. Tell me you do feel the same way about me.'

'I do. I've loved you since I was seventeen. After a holiday in Scotland my parents and I were staying one night in Dundale, and we went to a village concert—'

He laughed as he thought back to his youth. 'Now I remember,' he said wonderingly. 'You were the loveliest thing I'd ever seen…' He kissed her deeply. 'I dreamt about you for months, and bitterly regretted not taking the chance to talk to you, but my then girlfriend had been with me. But I remembered that night for years…'

He kissed her passionately, then observed, 'Fate works in mysterious ways. Once you were just a beautiful face that haunted me, now you're my wife…'

'Well, not quite,' she said demurely and, getting off his knee, took his hand. 'But I'm sure we could remedy that.'

Laughing, he rose to his feet and swept her up in his arms. 'We could indeed, my love.'

REQUEST YOUR FREE BOOKS!

2 FREE NOVELS PLUS 2 FREE GIFTS!

HARLEQUIN®

Blaze®

Red-hot reads!

YES! Please send me 2 FREE Harlequin® Blaze® novels and my 2 FREE gifts. After receiving them, if I don't wish to receive any more books, I can return the shipping statement marked "cancel." If I don't cancel, I will receive 6 brand-new novels every month and be billed just $3.99 per book in the U.S., or $4.47 per book in Canada, plus 25¢ shipping and handling per book and applicable taxes, if any*. That's a savings of at least 15% off the cover price! I understand that accepting the 2 free books and gifts places me under no obligation to buy anything. I can always return a shipment and cancel at any time. Even if I never buy another book from Harlequin, the two free books and gifts are mine to keep forever.

151 HDN EF3W 351 HDN EF3X

Name _____ (PLEASE PRINT)

Address _____ Apt. _____

City _____ State/Prov. _____ Zip/Postal Code _____

Signature (if under 18, a parent or guardian must sign)

Mail to Harlequin Reader Service®:

IN U.S.A.
P.O. Box 1867
Buffalo, NY
14240-1867

IN CANADA
P.O. Box 609
Fort Erie, Ontario
L2A 5X3

Not valid to current Harlequin Blaze subscribers.

Want to try two free books from another line?
Call 1-800-873-8635 or visit www.morefreebooks.com.

* Terms and prices subject to change without notice. NY residents add applicable sales tax. Canadian residents will be charged applicable provincial taxes and GST. This offer is limited to one order per household. All orders subject to approval. Credit or debit balances in a customer's account(s) may be offset by any other outstanding balance owed by or to the customer. Please allow 4 to 6 weeks for delivery.

HB06